THE HOLEY LAND

THE SECOND ADDISON J. FREEMAN STORY

A NOVEL BY

J. J. ZERR

PRIMIX
PUBLISHING
THE WRITE CHOICE

Primix Publishing
11620 Wilshire Blvd
Suite 900, West Wilshire Center, Los Angeles, CA, 90025
www.primixpublishing.com
Phone: 1-800-538-5788

Published by Primix Publishing: 01/08/2024

ISBN: 979-8-89194-023-9(sc)
ISBN: 979-8-89194-024-6(hc)
ISBN: 979-8-89194-025-3(e)

Library of Congress Control Number: 2023919788

THE HOLEY LAND

CONTENTS

1860

God bless editors and my buds
of Coffee and Critique.

1860

Percy clip-clopped along the baked, hard-packed dirt of Main Street. Addison J. Freeman sat on the buggy's driver bench, holding the reins in his left hand. With his right, he pulled the pistol from the shoulder holster on his left side and pointed it straight ahead, at nothing. Replacing the handgun, and pausing for a clip, clop, he drew again. A little faster this time.

"When it's time fer shootin"—according to Joshua Reedley, wagon master during the Holy Crusade from Illinois to Kansas—"a little faster makes a lotta difference." And he always added, "A little straighter makes a lotta difference, too."

The wagon master, more of a father to Addison than his pa had been.

And Percy. Addison still thought of him as Percy-the-pony, though the animal was old enough to be called Percy-the-grandpa. He could still pull a wagon, though. If the land were Kansas flat. If the wagon were empty. If there was no snow on the ground.

No snow on the ground this morning.

The last snow had been back in February. Since then, Kansas and the town of Brotherton had not been kissed by a single drop of moisture from the sky. Drought baked the land, the people, and the animals. Behind Addison, the big egg yolk was only halfway up to noon high, but it was noontime hot already and then some. The heat of the sun sat heavy on his shoulders like the meaty hands of a blacksmith.

The horse didn't seem to mind the heat. He seemed glad to get out of the small pen at the rear of the two-horse shed behind Addison's and Mariah's house at the east end of Main.

To Addison, the town of Brotherton went up as if by a miracle. During the fall, most of the men and a few women had been assigned to Otto Vogelsang's crew of carpenters. They erected the Meeting House, the church, and a huge communal barn in the center of the town layout, while most of the women and a few of the men planted winter wheat.

In late fall, with the planting done, every able-bodied person was put to work building family dwellings. With each building they set up, the crew got better and faster at their jobs, and Otto hollered German at them less and less.

When the congregation of Found Grace church from northeastern Illinois arrived here late in 1858, a man could stand where Main Street was now and look north and see nothing but prairie grass. A half mile to the south, the buildings around Pott's Trading Post rose above the plain. Beyond that, though, there was no sign of civilization for forty miles to Prairietown.

Now, in the space of nine months, Brotherton stood, looking solid and as if it had been there for years. Otto had laid out the town with German precision and orderliness. Main, Second, Third, and up to a Sixth Street ran east/west. He did not want to vaste time naming the north/south running cross streets, so he called them A, B, C, and D Streets. Otto had placed six houses on the west half of each numbered street, and six more on the eastern halves. Behind each house there was room for a garden and sheds. His plan kept all the citizens close together for mutual protection. If the families had lived in scattered farmhouses, the pro-slavers would have had an easy time of wiping them out one by one.

So far, only a half dozen houses sat on Fifth Street. If more free-state voters showed up, Otto would build houses for them.

The winter wheat crop had not yielded what the Crusaders had hoped for because of the drought. At present, many of the men spent their days hauling water from the Delaware River to town to keep vegetable gardens, one cornfield, and one field of oats alive.

The drought concerned the Town Council. They'd hoped Brotherton would be well on the way to self-sufficiency by this point, halfway through 1859.

During the early months of this year, most of the people of Brotherton praised the Vogelsang building crews. Now though, a few surly voices grumbled, "The stupid Deutcher forgot to plant a single shade tree anywhere in town."

Mayor Gallant Argyl said, "Just like we had to fight our way here, we have to fight to stay here. We will survive if we work together. We are all in the same boat here. Bellyaching is wasted effort. If you complain, it means we haven't given you enough work to do."

Preacher Larrimer proclaimed, "In Kansas, we are engaged in the Lord's work. We've come through hardships, and more face us every day. But our God is with us. The Israelites grumbled against God while in the desert. In doing so, they sinned. Grumbling here in Brotherton, in New Found Grace Church, commits the same sin the Jewish people committed. Rather than grumbling, trust in God. And thank Him.

"If we but look back to when our Holy Crusade crossed Illinois and Missouri, we will see the hand of the Lord God helping us, saving us from danger every step along the way.

"Be ever thankful," his voice boomed out his conclusion, "Be never belly-aching."

After he'd delivered that sermon, if he heard complaining, the grumbler would do a stint on the penance pew in the front of church, and he would confess his sin every day to the congregation until the preacher thought his confession was sincere.

Percy slowed to a walk and jerked Addison out of his reverie back to Main Street. Joshua Reedley would have said, "Jerked your head outta where it shouldn't be to back on your shoulders where it should be all the time!" He also said, "Women say their work is never done, but neether is a scout's. You don't keep your mind on your business every minute, you will be a dead scout."

During that wagon train trip across Illinois, Mr. Reedley had turned Addison from a teenage kid into a nineteen-year-old man who could kill other men if they threatened the Crusaders.

Addison knew he let his mind, let his head wander to where it shouldn't be. It was hard, what with being married, and he and Mariah owning their own house to shelter them and their daughter Hope. It just felt … safe there in the miracle town of Brotherton.

Without needing a tug on the reins, the horse turned onto B Street heading north, past the Meeting House. Addison did tug on the reins to turn onto Second, and he whoa-ed Percy very close to the front of the church.

Marvin Dinwiddie and Fred Fishboch waited for him there on the yard-wide boardwalk in front of the church. The two of them, along with Addison and Norm Niedlinger, who manned a lookout post in the belltower, had been assigned to the Brotherton Citizens Safety Committee for the day. They were responsible for guarding Brotherton and ringing the church bell to summon aid if a significant threat showed up. The rest of the men and women worked the fields or carted water or taught school or tended the children too young to work.

The committee was responsible for was guarding the town, but Addison decided they could meet that responsibility as well as mount the cross on the church bell tower. The top of the house of worship was the ideal lookout spot.

Otto Vogelsang planned to install the cross that evening, before sunset.

Addison intended to surprise the builder. He sent Sam and Fred up onto the roof of the belltower and told them to take a rope, and to, "Take your guns with you."

The long guns would be awkward to manage up there, but Safety Committee members were to be always armed. Always.

Addison lifted a ladder from the wagon bed and placed the base of it atop an empty crate in the wagon to turn a short ladder into a longer one. He carried the cross from inside the church to outside, tied the rope to it, and hollered, "Hoist 'er up. Careful, though. We don't want a banged-up cross on top of New Found Grace Church."

As the cross rose slowly, Addison climbed his longer ladder with the cross resting on his back. When his feet reached the second last rung, he decided he should not go higher. "Can you reach it, Norm?"

"Yeah—"

"Vott you Idiots doin?" Otto Vogelsang.

"Um," Addison said. He was in no position to turn around. "We're putting the cross atop the belltower."

"Nein. You dumbkopfs trying to kill stupid selfs! Addison, you come down."

Addison thought about it. Otto was not a member of the Town Council. He'd been invited but said he did not have time for such foolishness when there were houses to build.

"In a minute," Addison said. "Norm, haul the cross up onto the church roof."

"Stop! "Lower cross to ground."

"No, Mr. Vogelsang. Now, Norm, haul the cross up."

Norm hauled it up and laid it on the sloping roof. Then he looked to the southeast. "Rider coming. From the River ferry lookout post, I think. Alphonse Carlson."

Alphonse manned the Delaware River ferry crossing sentry post with Peggy Argyl. It was a fording spot now with the river being low due to the drought.

"All you dumbkopfs, come down. Now!"

"No, Mr. Vogelsang. Norm, stay where you are. Stay alert. Sam and Fred, you stay up there on the belltower roof."

Sam said, "Yes, Sir."

Yes, Sir? Sam was nineteen, a year younger than Addison. Their experiences last year had been very different, however. Sam had ridden with the wagon train while Addison had scouted in front. Sam hadn't killed anyone. Addison had killed. Sam was a bachelor. Addison was married, owned a farm, and had a daughter. But yes, sir?

"Come down from ladder, Idiot! Or maybe you no understand English needer!"

Mr. Vogelsang was getting pretty excited. If he spooked Percy into taking a step, Addison would fall more than ten feet. Before descending, he glanced left, to the west. Nothing moved. Just desert-hot haze hiding the horizon. As he started down, the builder continued to rant.

"I build whole town and no man hurt. Not even get splinter in finger. Now, idiots climb ladders like … like … dat!"

Addison stepped onto the crate and hopped to the bed. Percy took a step. The wagon lurched, and the ladder started falling. Addison caught it, laid it in the bed, jumped to the ground, and strode across Second Street to where the builder stood with bunched fists on his hips.

Otto Vogelsang was a good two inches taller and a good one hundred pounds heavier, but Addison stomped right up to him and glared up into his face. "I was stupid on the ladder. You were stupid on the ground. All your hollering spooked the horse."

"If your vater here, he switch you good."

"He'd try," Addison replied.

Growing up, Addison had received a goodly number of switchings from his pa. The last one was last year.

Just then, Alphonse Carlson reined up in the middle of Second Street. "Ziggy Hostetler's crossing the river with nine supply wagons. He wants to speak with the Town Council."

"Ride out to Sixth Street and notify the mayor and the preacher," Addison ordered the sentry.

"I have to get back to my post."

"Were any of Ziggy's wagons across the river when you left?" Addison said.

"Two of them."

"Then your sentry post is secure. Go find the mayor, like I said."

Alphonse reined around and headed north down B Street.

"You make a good scout, Addison. And a good deputy marshal.

But maybe you should let the carpentering to us Vogelsangs."
Hermann, Otto's son, smirked.

"Then perhaps, Hermann, you should climb onto the roof and show the guys up there how to install the cross the Vogelsang way." Said without a smirk.

Addison entered the add-on kitchen built onto the west side of the Meeting House.

The windows and doors were open, but the heat inside was stifling. A breeze would have helped, however the drought seemed to have fried the life out of the everlasting west wind. According to the people at Pott's Trading Post, that unceasing wind whistling over the prairie night and day had driven some people mad. Now, the everlasting heat was maddening.

Frieda Grossman stuck a piece of kindling into the cooking stove, closed the firebox door, and smiled at Addison. She was engaged to Charlie McTavish, son of the town marshal. She wore a short-sleeved blouse scooped low in front and back. The top hung loose over a split skirt. Mrs. Larrimer had okayed such clothing for the cooks.

Early during the Holy Crusade, some of the women had worn split skirts to enable riding astride, instead of side-saddle, into a hostile town. The split-skirt women had also been armed. Joshua Reedley had figured the men of the town would be reluctant to shoot women, whereas they would not have hesitated to gun down Abolitionist men. The Wagon Master had been right.

Addison had gotten used to seeing women wear those split skirts, but that low scooped blouse drew his eyes like horseshoe nails to a magnet.

"We have cool water in the cellar," Frieda said.

He made himself look her in the eye. "Coffee for now, please. And, Frieda, the Town Council will be meeting here soon."

She poured coffee into a tin cup and handed it to him. "I'll put on another pot, then."

Addison entered the Meeting House. It was noticeably … less hot than in the kitchen.

On the Second Street end of the building, six baby cribs filled the right corner. A young woman changed a baby's napkin at a table. Another young woman sat on a chair against the wall and knitted. His daughter, Hope, slept in one of the two occupied beds. He smiled down upon her.

The other corner of the Meeting House was walled off. Addison's wife, Mariah, used that space for her healing work.

When the Holy Crusade had arrived in a small town in central Illinois, the pastor of the church hosted Preacher Larrimer and his community. Mariah, and her parents, and four other families from that town had joined the wagon train. In her community, they called Mariah The Healer. Mariah's father had told the Wagon Master, Reedley, that healing was just short of doctoring. Preacher Larrimer proclaimed such medical abilities manifested in one so young to be, clearly, a gift from God. Addison had seen her that way, too, albeit for another reason. He found her attractive.

By the time the Crusade reached the Mississippi River, Mariah had treated cuts, broken arms, dysentery, and a problem pregnancy. At a Sunday service, Preacher Larrimer proclaimed a booming, "Thank You, Almighty God and Father, for blessing our Crusade with Mariah The Healer. Only You know how much we need her to ensure we all of us arrived safely in Kansas. Where we will vote to bring Kansas into the Union a free state, rather than another that sanctions the abomination that is slavery. Kansas, where we will vote to save the state from being accursed, and rather, make of it a Holy Land."

Lately, Mariah had begun to recall that sermon, and in their bedroom at night, she would hiss, "Holy Land the preacher called

Kansas. The newspapers call it Bleeding Kansas. And instead of Holy, I call it H-O-L-E-Y. Full of bullet holes."

Always, after such an outburst, whispered so as not to disturb their baby Hope, asleep in her cradle at the foot of their bed, Mariah would pull Addison tightly to her and weep silently. Once she'd whispered, "I'm afraid I'm going to lose you. Whenever there's shooting, you're in the middle of it."

He'd almost responded, "It's not that bad." But he'd kept his mouth shut and held her as she shed some of her fear in tears.

The sound of hammering obliterated his recollection. It came from the church. Hermann nailing the cross to the belltower.

Addison wanted to see his wife, but her door was closed.

The Meeting House had curtains that could be drawn, separating the large chamber into smaller rooms. Addison finished his coffee and pulled the two sides of floor-to-top-of-the-walls drapes together, separating the third of the space fronting Main Street. Then he pushed two tables together and placed chairs on both sides.

"Ad!" came from behind him.

"Zig," Addison replied before he turned around.

Ziggy Hostetler believed that many times, saying a name with more than one syllable could cost a man his life. He ran a freight-hauling business carting supplies from Atchison to Brotherton, Pott's Trading Post, the general store in Prairie Town, and sometimes all the way to Lawrence. On a number of those trips, he'd had to fight off ambushers to complete his journey.

Addison was used to seeing Ziggy as a mop of black hair with two shiny black eyes peering out from under his hat brim. The man now standing in the doorway held a flop-brimmed hat and was bald on top and clean-shaven. A thick, furry black pelt covered his forearms as if to make up for the lack of hair elsewhere.

"You get scalped?" Addison said.

"Nope. Sun burnt it off."

"Coffee or something to eat?"

"Yep and yep."

Ziggy's eyebrows levitated when Frieda walked through the

curtain carrying a tray loaded with coffee mugs and glasses. "Oh," Frieda said, "I didn't expect anyone to be here yet."

"Mr. Hostetler," Addison said, "it's hot enough in the kitchen to make a blacksmith faint." He hoped that was explanation enough for her dress, and he turned to Frieda. "A bowl of stew for our guest, please?"

"A glass of cool water from the cellar?" she said.

"Coffee. Ain't never too hot for not-on-the-trail-no-more coffee."

When she slipped back through the curtains, Ziggy's head twitched. "Jist used to seein' Brotherton wimmin buttoned up to their Eve's apple."

Trace chains jangled, and wagons rumbled past the open door and turned down C Street.

Thelma Tanber, one of the two tending the infants, pushed through and placed stew and coffee in front of Ziggy. Thelma wore a top buttoned at her throat.

Ziggy stared at her. Addison thanked her, and she left.

"Her sleeves were rolled up," Zig said. "Her bare elbows felt like seeing something forbidden." Then Zig dug into the stew.

Through the open windows, horse and buggy sounds from B Street announced the arrival of the town council. The preacher, mayor, marshal, and row bosses comprised Brotherton's governing body.

The row boss term held over from when the Crusade arrived. Then, the wagons had been lined up with twelve wagons side-by-side on what now was Main Street. Behind this dozen, another dozen, and beyond that, still another. A row boss had been appointed to manage each group of wagon's communal affairs. After Otto Vogelsang filled the first two streets with houses, someone suggested that row boss be changed to street boss, but no one liked the new term. Everyone, except the new name proposer, liked the old one.

With the council assembled, Ziggy told them that supplies for the Brotherton community filled his entire wagon train. The Emigrant Aid Society worried the drought might jeopardize the settlement's survival through the next winter and, so, had paid for the supplies.

He hadn't sent word those materials were coming because if the pro-slavers heard what was in his wagons, Ziggy was certain to be attacked somewhere between Atchison and Brotherton. If he transported goods for the trading post or the general store in Prairietown, the anti-Abolitionists left his wagons alone. He'd let it be known that he carried material for Pott's Trading Post on the present train, and that his next one would reprovision the general store in Prairietown.

"The Emigrant Aid Society," Preacher Larrimer said. "A true blessing from God. When are you leaving, Mr. Hostetler? I'd like you to carry a letter to the Society thanking them."

"Soon as we can, Preacher," Zig said. "I'll leave the wagons and animals with you. If you don't need 'em, sell 'em to the trading post. I will need saddle broncs for my men and provisions for an overnight on the trail."

"Won't take long to round those up," Marshal McTavish said.

"Nuther thing," Zig said. "Need Addison Freeman and Jibway Jim and four other men who kin fight."

"I thought you let it be known your next trip would carry freight for Prairietown," said Mrs. Freeman, Addison's mother, and Row One Boss.

"Yes'um. I put that word out. But when we depart the wagon train staging lot, we'll have fourteen wagons full of new free-staters to join you. They're probably at the wagon train staging lot now. Anyway, them pro-slavers are always watching me. They'll know I lied and have time to roust up a gang to attack us before we can get back here."

"Fourteen," said Joshua Reedley, Row Six Boss. "Otto's got some houses to build. Some even on my street."

"Kin I have them men I asked fer?" Zig said.

"No!" Mariah Freeman stood in the gap between the curtains.

Addison's ma started to get up.

"I'll talk to her, Ma," Addison said. He nodded once to Zig. Zig nodded back.

All eyes at the table were on Mariah. Those stares shifted to him as he rose and hurried to his wife.

"Mariah. Come outside with me? Please." He carefully avoided touching her, though she just stood there with her face buried in her hands. "Please?"

She spun about, stomped across the hall, through the kitchen, and out onto C Street. Addison hustled to keep up. He almost plowed into the back of her when she stopped abruptly at the corner of Second and B Streets.

*****

When he found out about Otto Vogelsang's water wagons, Zig asked for the loan of one of those also. Along the trail to Atchison, a number of the smaller creeks had dried up. The water tank would help the trip to Atchison, and the one back here, go a little quicker and a lot less thirsty.

Joshua Reedley volunteered to be one of the four men to go with Zig. Zig was pleased. Otto Vogelsang was not.

"Reedley good wagon master," Otto said. "Also, he, und Hermann, best builders I got. Vee got houses to build."

"Yes, Otto," Preacher Larrimer said. "But we need to get our new brothers here safely, or the new houses won't be needed."

"Yah, yah. Und dat Addison, he say we need to put new sentry post to west. Vee never have attack come from that direction. Und, it take two more workers away from me."

David McTavish said, "Our number one priority is to protect the Brotherton you built for us, Otto. And Addison is right. We have to expect the pro-slavers learned it is hard to get to us from the east and south. To the north is Indian territory. What's left?"

"Our second priority is hauling water," Mayor Gallant Argyl said. "That should leave you with enough of a crew to build one house. When the new settlers get here, they will have to do what we did. Live in their wagons for a while. Plus, they will bring additional laborers."

Addison pushed through the curtains and returned to his chair.

Marshal McTavish cleared his throat. "That concludes Town Council business. Preacher, would you lead us in prayer, please?"

W hen Addison was away, Mrs. Freeman stayed with her daughter-in-law and granddaughter. Mariah appreciated her husband's mother. A wonderful, resourceful, generous woman. And forgiving. She knew Mariah had gotten in the family way by Orson Seiling, a married man, but Addison had married her anyway, and Mrs. Freeman treated her daughter-in-law as if there was nothing at all untoward about the woman her son had chosen to wed.

Mariah knew her husband to be good and noble. Sprung from a good and noble woman.

She considered Addison's pa, however, a former deacon in Preacher 's church, to be close-minded, opinionated, and ready with a switch to inflict physical mortification on his only child for perceived sins. Mariah felt the scars from the switchings on her husband's back when they were in bed.

Thank You, Father, that Addison takes after his mother.

The preacher had removed Addison's pa's deacon status after he had challenged Larrimer for the spiritual and moral leadership of the Holy Crusaders. Disgraced Adolph Freeman then joined a wagon train headed for Oregon, or maybe it was Sante Fe.

Mrs. Freeman made no excuses for her husband, but she did pray that on his journey he'd find salvation and the goodness in his heart that he'd encased in a turtle shell of arrogance. Yes, Ma was a good, noble, and forgiving woman.

Mariah heated dinner over an outside fire under a canvas awning hung from the side of the house and propped on poles. A picnic table adorned with two place settings also rested under the sunshade. Hope, in a basket, sat on the table as well.

Mrs. Freeman washed her hands in the basin on the stand next to the house. After returning the towel to the nail, she walked to the table and watched her granddaughter. "Always love when babies discover they have hands."

"Mrs. Freeman," Mariah said, "thank you for staying with us when … when—"

"When he leaves you again," her mother-in-law finished for her. "You know, Dearest Daughter, that you must use your healing gift to serve our community. Do you not see that Addison, too, has a gift, and that this community depends on his ability to serve as a protector of us all?"

Preacher had told Mariah the same thing. As did Joshua Reedley and Marshal McTavish. Now that Mrs. Freeman said those words, they finally made sense. And she could accept them.

Mariah's parents lived in a house on Fourth Street. Close, but at the same time, far. Addison's ma had become her ma, too. More so than the woman who bore her.

Mrs. Freeman said, "I know you have heard our preacher say that God gives special talents to some so that those abilities may be used to serve their community."

Mariah had heard preachers say that a number of times, but once again, when voiced by her mother-in-law, it stuck, rather than the in-one-ear-and-out-the-other way it happened with sermons.

All too often. Forgive me, Father, I have sinned.

Thinking about her sins, she almost missed, "The greatest blessing I have received is to see the fingermarks of God on your back and on Addison's. From when He nudged you two together."

This conversation warmed Mariah, without making her hotter, and the feeling abided with her until she climbed into bed, rolled onto her side, and reached for her husband, for where he slept. When he was home.

*****

Joshua Reedley picked five men, including Addison and Jibway, to form a scouting party to ride in advance of Ziggy's group. Just after sunup, the scouts arrived at a stream with water in it. Reedley called a halt. The men watered their horses, then led them several yards away from the crossing, both north and south, where there was grass. Next the crossing, the grass had been chewed off to the roots. Two of them stayed awake, on watch. The others slept.

Ziggy'd ride a saddle bronc if he had to, but on this return trip to Atchison, he had the water wagon to drive. Thirteen mounted men and one spare horse rode with him. Ziggy pushed them through the afternoon and all night until mid-morning, when they caught up with Reedley's crew.

Addison and his blood brother, Jibway Jim, were on watch. They waited in the shade of trees along the banks of the stream. Reedley and the others slept.

To the west, ghost images of a wagon and riders emerged from the heat hazed distance. Zig drove the wagon on the side of the wheel and hoof scoured-of-grass and baked hard road. The water wagon would make less noise there. A little less noise. The dirt under the brown grass was as hard as a brick. Along the side of the road, though, there were fewer ruts sun-frozen into the roadway.

The horses around the water wagon stepped up the pace. The smell of water enough to overpower the fatigue of hours and hours of carrying a man or pulling a wagon. Reedley and his three men sat up, roused by the hooves clopping and trace chains jangling.

Addison saw Ziggy startle awake. He didn't have reins in hand. His team took to the center of the roadway. Trees and saplings along the stream hemmed in the crossing to two wagon widths. The team stopped with forelegs in water, and, as one, bent their necks to drink.

Ziggy's riders fanned out around him and pushed through brush and saplings to get to the stream.

Reedley said, "There's graze along the banks, but you gotta go coupla hundred yards up or down stream. Reckon you know that, Zig."

Zig nodded.

After the horses got their first bellyful of water, the men moved them to where the banks of the stream held green grass that hadn't been chewed to the roots. Half went north. The other half moved south. There they hobbled their animals, ate a fireless meal, and flopped onto their bedrolls.

Joshua Reedley deployed Jibway to scout east, Addison to head south, and his other two men to establish a lookout post two miles back toward Brotherton. He would scout north. Ziggy and his party, except for two always on watch, would sleep there next to the stream.

*****

It's always darkest before the dawn. When the sun comes up, it'll get better.

Mariah had always believed that. Before the Holy Crusade brought her to Bleeding Kansas. Now, before the sun rose, the pro- and anti-slavery sides slept on, exhausted from yesterday's battles of survival and extermination. After the first fiery sliver crested the edge of the world, the warriors for both sides would rise and check the loads in their guns. Shortly, there'd be more bleeding in Kansas.

The lamp on the kitchen table created a tiny dawn all her own as Mariah sat in the rocker nursing three-month-old Hope. Hope stopped sucking and opened her eyes, and baby eyes stabbed mother heart with so much love it hurt. After a moment, the slice of ache transformed into a chestful of warmth.

"Such a treasure you are, little … no, not little Hope. You are tiny and the biggest of all blessings at the same time." *Thank You, Father God of heaven and earth.*

Hope continued to feed, eyes closed again, as if she couldn't be bothered by all that philosophical folderol. Mariah smiled. That blessed moment of soul-to-soul contact with the fruit of her womb wiped away those other, harsher, even brutal times of each day.

For a moment.

Mariah and Addison had talked about how 1859 would be so much better. The Crusaders would build their new town, and the constant need to fight for survival would be behind them. It had not turned out that way, however. The town of Brotherton had been built and was still expanding, but the pro-slavery forces remained bent on the extinction of the Abolitionists.

Abolitionist. Said with such loathing, as if it were the most repulsive word in the English language. Preacher said slavery was an abomination, and the pro-slavers were Abominationists. And Brotherton's hate-driven adversaries were persistent. Over the last seven months, there had been four raids, all of which had been thwarted because of the vigilance of the people of Brotherton.

Hope finished on one side, and Mariah hoisted the baby onto the spit up rag on her shoulder and patted the baby's back.

"Oh, you are such a good burper! Yes, you are."

After settling the baby on the other side, Mariah's mind went to her husband.

He was a wonderful man. His soul was clean and pure.

Not like Orson Seiling. She'd been such a fool to fall for him and his charm after her family joined the Holy Crusade wagon train in central Illinois. She hadn't known he was married when she lay with him. After, she'd expected him to marry her. He never asked her that, though he continued to ask her to sneak away from the wagons with him at night. Just before the wagon train had reached the Mississippi River, she asked him to marry her. He stopped unbuttoning her dress and told her about being married to Lizbeth.

The betrayal stunned her, petrified her. Orson undid another of her buttons, and white-hot fury blazed up out of her chest and filled her head. She'd slapped him, again, and again. He caught her wrists and held her until she collapsed to the ground sobbing. After a sleepless night, a case of diarrhea, a broken finger, and blistered hand from a hot skillet called her to her duties as healer.

Shortly after the Crusaders arrived at the site of what became Brotherton, Mariah discovered she was pregnant. She told Orson. Orson told Addison. The next day, Orson sported a black eye and a fat lip. The day after that, Addison told Mariah they should get married.

"But I don't'—" She'd intended to say, "I don't love you," but he cut her off. "I love you enough for the three of us," he said as he placed his hand on her stomach.

Now, she told Addison every morning and every night that she loved him with all her heart and all her soul.

Well. She told him when he was home.

Hope fussed. She'd lost the nipple. Mariah got the baby reattached.

Addison. Incredible how they came to be married.

"It shows you how much God wants us to be together," he'd told her.

If He wants us to be together, why are you gone all the time, Addison J. Freeman?

This time he'd gone to Atchison to guide another Emigrant Aid Society wagon train to Brotherton. The new group of settlers would bring the number of families in the settlement to more than fifty. Many of these families traveled all the way from the east coast on their holy crusades. The pro-slavery Abominationists only had to cross the Missouri/Kansas Territory border.

At times, it seemed as if the Holy Crusaders were losing the battle to make the anti-slavery population larger than the pro-slavery. And the pro-slavery forces seemed to have all the legal advantages. Sheriffs in the regions around Leavenworth were pro-slavery. The sheriff in Prairietown between Brotherton and Lawrence was pro-slavery.

There had been so much violence between the two factions that the US Army had been tasked with restoring law and order. As the sheriffs were duly constituted legal authority, the army sided with them.

They'd had such hope as 1859 began. That's why their baby bore the name she did. And she was their baby. She had been ever since Addison first laid his hand on her stomach.

But he was gone more than he was home. Guiding wagon trains or protecting Brotherton from pro-slavery murderers. She missed him but feared for him more. He'd been involved in gun battles on some of his … missions, and she probably didn't know how many times he'd had to kill or be killed.

The door to the second bedroom opened. Addison's mother entered the big room. She was dressed for the day. "A blessed morning to the two of you."

"And to you, Mrs. Freeman."

The elder Mrs. Freeman said, "Father God of heaven and earth, watch over Addison and all our men on the journey to and from Atchison."

The younger amen-ed.

"About finished?" from Grandma.

"She's asleep."

"And she'd like to stay just like that for another couple hours. Wouldn't you, Little Princess?"

Grandma took the spit-up rag from Mariah and draped it on her own shoulder. Mariah eased the baby from her. Hope's contented face scrunched into a frown. Her tiny fists waved. But before the baby cried, Addison's mother took her and placed her over her shoulder and cooed and paced and patted.

Before Mariah entered her bedroom, the burp sounded. The lusty burp elicited a Thank You, Father God in heaven, my—our—baby is healthy. It was always important to bestow paternity on her husband. In a way, it was like her mother-in-law was more mother to her than her own parent.

She completed her morning prayers while dressing quickly. Then she hurried outside and stood still on the porch and listened and probed with all her senses for signs of danger. Their house was the eastern most one on Main Street. East. Pro-slavers came from there. Detecting no hint of threat, she strode to the barn and harnessed Percy to the buggy, and all the while, her senses tingled. The very air seemed so charged with menace that when she'd reached for the horse collar from the peg, a spark zapped from her finger to a metal ring on the collar.

Mariah had moments of peace throughout the days when Addison was gone, but the sense of threat from the east never ceased to find an opportunity to rush, or creep, back into her awareness.

The first time Addison left on one of his missions after Hope was born, Mariah was so gripped by fear, she'd tried to nurse Hope, but her milk wouldn't let down. Thank You, God, Ma Freeman was there. They prayed together. "Give your fear to our Father in heaven," her mother-in-law said. "Just give it to Him and let it go." They prayed and talked some more, and then Hope had breakfast.

That same night with the baby asleep and the two women washing supper dishes, Mariah said, "I asked the Lord to take my fear. He took some of it, but a lot remains."

Ma Freeman smiled. "Dearest Daughter, God has been answering prayers since creation. If He left some fear remain with you, it was because it is better for you than if He took it all."

Mariah stopped scrubbing the plate, stared at the blank wall in front of her for a moment, said, "Oh," dunked the soapy plate in the pan of rinse water, then passed the plate to her mother-in-law.

When the Hostetler party headed east again an hour before sunset, Addison and Jibway scouted two miles in front. During the night, nothing threatened the travelers. Sunrise found them two hours short of the wagon train staging lot. A succession of farms began lining the road and herding the two scouts onto it.

Jibway scowled at the sliver of sun peeking above the horizon. "I hate this! An Indian would not ride into a sunrise if there were any hint of a threat. He'd wait. A white man says, 'We're burning daylight.' He says, 'Giddy up.' The sun blinds scouts. The wind is from the west. When we head east, we are blind, and our horses can't smell a pro-slaver ambush."

Addison's astonishment obviously showed.

"What?" Jibway said. "You're surprised I speak your language better than you do?"

"Well, yeah. What was with that ... that—"

"Injun talk?" Jibway offered.

"Yeah. That."

"When I started working for Mr. Hostetler, some of his men thought I was acting uppity when I spoke the way I learned to speak in missionary school. Some of them picked fights with me. They wound up getting hurt. Ziggy asked me if I'd talk more Injun like.

"How,' I said, and he showed me. He pays me more than he pays the white guys, so I do it to keep his workers from getting hurt."

"Huh," Addison said as Jibway cantered his mount ahead. Outlaw knew to trail the other horse by fifty yards. Scouting down a road, riding into the sun, the lead rider was most at risk. But, if the lead ran into an ambush, the other scout could ride back and warn the wagon train. When Addison scouted with others, he always took the lead position. With his blood brother, they switched off riding the highest risk spot.

There were a lot of things Addison didn't tell Mariah about what he did when he was away from her. That was one of them.

The sun peeked above the edge of the world. Like a bird. When it hears a sound and raises its head just enough for an eyeball to peek over the edge of the nest to determine if it needs to fly away. In addition to the brightening sky, lamp glow through farmhouse kitchen windows dotted both sides of the road.

Here, the farmers were not afraid to live separated from the nearest town.

"Someday, Brotherton will be this civilized, eh, Outlaw?" Addison said to his horse. The animal bobbed his head.

Jibway slowed. Addison caught up. They rode side-by-side for a moment. Addison said, "When a scout thinks he's safe, he watches more carefully, not less."

One of Jibway's "words to live by."

"Huh," Jibway said. "Yesterday, Jibway say, 'Addison J. Freeman. He be half Injun.' Now Jibway say, 'He be two-thirds Injun.'"

*****

The wagon train staging lot on the western edge of Atchison was jammed full. Addison found the lot manager, Norb Bass, cussing and fuming at four men clustered outside his shack on the north side of the lot.

"Y'all keep adding wagons to your trains. We ain't got room for the ones we already got stuffed in here. Mr. Warren, you been here the longest. You're going to have to move your train out."

"I ain't leavin'," Warren said. "We ain't headin' west till the drought lifts. All we'd be doin' is burying the women and kids. Sides. Why we gotta' go? Make the latecomers leave."

Bass took a deep breath, huffed it out, and nodded. One of his men stuck a pistol in Warren's back as another removed the man's two pistols and a boot gun.

"Tie him up and throw him in the shack," Norb said.

Warren started cussing.

"And gag him. We got women and kids here."

Warren was forced to move his twenty-five wagons east, back across the Missouri River. There was space and water there to host a passel of wagons, while around Atchison, besides the staging lot, there was no place with ample water for the people and animals of a wagon train.

Norb spat tobacco juice. Some of it cleared his moustache. He turned to Addison. "East a the Missourah's where yore Emigrant Aid Society pilgrims is staged also."

"Jibway," Addison said, "How about riding back to Zig. Tell him and Joshua Reedley what's happening here. I'll cross the river and check on our new neighbors."

*****

The Missouri was low. Still, the river was not fordable. Addison and Outlaw arrived at the crossing with the raft at midstream headed for the west bank. The water coursing down the Missouri looked gray and gave the illusion of being solid enough to walk on. Behind him, wagons rumbled.

Two wagons, probably the first of Mr. Warren's train rattled on the rough road. On the first, a giant filled most of the driver bench. A normal-sized woman sat on the end of the bench with the reins in her hand. She tugged on them and whoa-ed the team about fifteen feet short of Addison. The Giant snatched the reins from her and snapped them across his team's backs. The wagon lurched forward, and Addison pushed Outlaw off the roadbed.

The Giant stopped his team just short of the water. He glared at Addison. "Boy, don't you never git in my way agin."

Addison stomped back to stand adjacent to the driver. "Mr. I got a warning for you, too. You crowd me like that again, and I'll shoot your horses."

"You ain't shootin' nothin' or nobody!" came from Addison's left.

A man almost as tall, almost as heavy as the giant strode up the side of the wagon. He had a cocked musket against his shoulder aimed at Addison. He kept coming. Addison figured he intended to jam the barrel into his chest.

Addison smashed his left hand against the musket barrel. It went off aiming at the sky. Then he drew his pistol from his shoulder holster, cocked it and aimed it at the big man on the driver bench as he drew his belt gun and aimed it at the one with the musket. "Ma'am, I don't want to hurt your men, but I don't aim to let them ride roughshod over me neither."

"They won't give you no more trouble, Mister." To the man beside her, "Tell him."

The Giant just glowered at Addison.

"Tell him you won't bother him, Zeke."

Zeke tore his hostile stare away from Addison and aimed it at the river. "I won't bother you."

"Ever again. Say that to the man."

"Mena! What if I gotta defend myself?"

"Bother means you started it. Again," Addison said. "It don't mean you can't defend yourself. That right, Ma'am."

She agreed. Zeke said what he was told to say. Addison offered his name to the woman. "Wilhelmina Little."

"Little?" Addison said.

The woman's face cracked, and a little smile broke through. "He's called L'il Zeke. Our boy is L'il Clem."

"Ma'am," Addison said. "I'd appreciate it if you'd wait and take the next raft across. Will you do that? It'll lessen the chance there'll be more trouble between us."

"Now see here—"

"Shut up, Zeke. If we went on the first raft with Mr. Freeman, clearly, it would bother him, and you just promised you wouldn't do that. We'll take the second."

The raft touched the riverbank. Raft-man loaded two wagons, Outlaw, plus five other saddle horses, two married couples, and seven young children. Raft-man assigned Addison and one of the husbands, Nathan Holder, to pull the float away from shore.

"Shame we don't have L'il Clem here to pull us across," Nathan said.

Addison stood in front of Nathan, smoothly hand-over-handing on the tow rope which ran through iron rings affixed to the top of posts fastened to the side of the raft.

"Wilhelmina been after Zeke. And her boy. 'Men out here have guns,' she told 'em. 'and they're quick to use them. Best you back off your pushy ways.'"

Nathan paused. An invitation to speak, Addison figured.

"'I got guns,' Zeke told her."

"She fired right back, 'Yeah, and that scares me even more. If you wanna git yourself killed, why you gist go right ahead, but I don't want anything to happen to my son.'"

Another pause. Addison didn't bite on this one either.

"Zeke said, 'He's my son, too.'"

"She said, 'You git yore fool-self killed, he'll by my son.'"

Nathan stopped putting small pauses in his narration to give Addison an opportunity to say something. A steady story of the Little family rolled out. At midstream, Raft-man and the other husband took over on the rope.

Addison hustled to the front of the raft, hoping like all get out Nathan wouldn't follow him. When he stood beside Outlaw, he turned. No Nathan. A phew escaped his lips. He turned back toward Missouri and tipped his hat to heaven.

*****

As soon as the raft touched the riverbank, Addison led Outlaw ashore and mounted. The ride to the wagon train staging lot was up a gentle rise and about a half mile.

The lot was situated on a bluff overlooking the Missouri River. Nine wagons had been parked at the overlook edge of the lot. A large tent stood at the far end. The sides were rolled up. Men, women, and children crowded the benches lined up before a preacher and his podium.

This tall, thin man of God had white hair and beard and wore a light gray suit. Still, he resembled Preacher Larrimer despite the latter's black hair and clothing.

This preacher said, "Blessed are they which are persecuted for righteousness' sake; theirs is the kingdom of heaven."

Both preachers spoke in rich baritones. Though Larrimer's voice boomed. This man's subdued words wafted on a breeze to his still-as-statue listeners.

"Blessed are ye, when men shall revile you, and shall say all manner of evil against you falsely, for My sake.

"Rejoice, and be exceeding glad, for great is your reward in heaven. For so they persecuted the prophets, which were before you."

The preacher lowered his head and held the pose. And held it.

None of those under the tent seemed to squirm or fidget. Addison did both.

The preacher raised his head and his arms toward heaven.

"Thank You, Jehovah, for the many blessings You bestowed on us this day."

Someone from the benches said, "And the day has just begun."

"Amen," they all said.

Then the preacher said, "We have a visitor."

It seemed as if the whole congregation turned on their seats and stared. The ones in the back, Addison could tell, were scared as all get out.

Addison dismounted, and as he led Outlaw toward the tent, the preacher hustled down the center aisle.

"I'm Addison Freeman, and I'm from Brotherton."

On the rear benches under the tent with the sides rolled up, the concern on the faces of the congregation visibly melted to profound relief.

Preacher Caleb Cromwell introduced himself and explained that not more than an hour ago, four armed men showed up, and they stole a wagon filled with provisions.

"Four!" Addison scanned the crowd and dismounted. "There's at least twenty adult men among you, and you let four thieves just ride in here and steal your provisions? Why didn't you stop them?"

"We of Faith, Hope, and Love Church do not believe in violence," the preacher replied.

"Welcome to this part of the world, Preacher Cromwell," Addison said. "A lot of people here do believe in violence, and they practice it every day."

The man of God's chin inched up toward heaven, and his chest puffed out. "We will not."

"Then," Addison said, "all of you will probably die."

Cromwell flinched. Men filed out from under the tent and lined up beside the preacher. A second row formed behind him.

The man to the Preacher's left wore a black suit, white shirt, and an equally white beard. He said, "If we have to die, then it is God's will that we do so."

In the back row, a clean-shaven young man, probably twenty, spoke. "And we not only accept God's will, we wholeheartedly embrace it."

Addison shook his head as he thought about how hard it would be to get these … these … innocents to Brotherton. And to keep them alive IF he got them there.

At the sound of wagons rumbling onto the staging lot, Addison turned.

Nathan Holder drove the lead wagon. Addison didn't know the driver of the second. Holder stopped his wagon next to Outlaw, set the brake, and wound the reins around the handle. "Who're these folks?" he said to Addison.

"They're all members of Faith, Hope, and Love Church," Addison said. "They'll be moving to Brotherton, Kansas. Where I'm from."

The driver of the second wagon walked up and stopped beside Nathan. "Kerwood Benfield."

Benfield carried a musket in his left hand. A little short of six feet tall. Smooth shaven. Dark brown eyes measured Addison. Then he stuck out his hand.

"Is there a staging lot boss?" Nathan said. "Like Norb Bass back across the river?"

Addison shook his head, then turned and nodded to the church people. "They got here yesterday." He explained where they were bound; and that they expected the rest of their wagons to be delivered that afternoon from Pott's Provisioners located in Atchison; that they were anti-violence; that this morning four robbers stole their wagon filled with provisions; and they didn't lift a finger to stop them.

Kerwood shook his head, disgust written on his face. "They look like sheep. They're looking at us like we're hungry wolves."

Addison introduced Nathan and Kerwood to Preacher Cromwell. Then he asked the preacher for a man to ride after the robbers with him.

"We will not lift a hand—"

"Yes, Preacher. I've been here for two minutes, and I know full well what kind of people you are. Now I need someone to show me which way the robbers went and to identify them if we can catch up to them."

"None of us will ride with you and help you murder those men."

Addison asked Kerwood if he'd ride with him after the robbers. Penfield pondered the question a moment, then he nodded.

"Nathan," Addison said. "Park yours and Benfield's wagons on the far side of the lot. I imagine the Littles' wagon will get here soon. Tell Mrs. Little I appointed her Lot Boss."

Figuring out which way the robbers went wasn't hard. At the base of the rise leading to the staging lot, a road lined with dense forest on both sides headed east away from the ferry landing. No way for a wagon to head either north or south.

Addison instructed Kerwood to position himself fifty yards behind and on the opposite side of the road from the one he and Outlaw took.

As Outlaw cantered, Addison felt moisture in the air. It seemed forever since moisture-laden air had touched his face and arms. Insect noises! Out on the drought-baked prairie those sounds had dried up, too. He swatted a mosquito. The one blessing from the drought. No mosquitoes. The path they followed was on river bottom land, probably inundated during spring floods. The smell of mold and mildew sat heavy on the air. Pushing his mind back to the task at hand, he checked behind him. Benfield. Right where he was supposed to be. Eyes back to the front. Ears tuned to detect threatening sounds between his horse's clips and clops. Not that he'd hear much with the crickets chirping, crows cawing, and a hawk's scree.

After they had traveled four miles, Addison spotted a tendril of smoke rising above the trees ahead. He motioned Benfield forward and pointed out the smoke to him. Then they moved on as before.

Alongside the road, the trees allowed grass to grow in some spots. Addison directed Outlaw onto the hoof muffling greenage.

He arrived at a spot where a trail cut off to his right. Standing beside Outlaw, he could hear voices. Benfield pulled up beside him and dismounted.

"Wait here," Addison said. "And hold your horse's nose to keep him from answering if the robber horses whiney at him." Then he pushed his way through the brush slowly and as quietly as he could.

After perhaps fifteen minutes, Addison spotted the top of a covered wagon. He smelled bacon. Easing closer, he saw three men sitting cross-legged around a fire with bacon sizzling and spitting in a large black skillet. One of the men stirred the meat around with a stick. Another took a long swallow out of a whiskey jug and then passed it. The third raised the jug and guzzled.

Addison drew both pistols and stepped from the brush into the clearing. "Sit right still."

Whiskey Jug Holder and Bacon Stirrer stared with their mouths open. The guy between them reached for his belt gun. Addison shot him before he had his pistol out of his holster.

Bacon Stirrer dropped the stick and drew his gun. Addison shot him, too.

The other dropped the jug to draw. The jug shattered. Addison shot him, and he fell backward. A rivulet of whiskey reached the fire and flared up. Flames followed the spilled booze and set the third man's pants on fire.

Addison holstered one gun and rolled Pants On Fire onto his face, smothering the flames. Then he called for Benfield. They ate the bacon and biscuits the robbers had laid out. Then they buried them in a single grave, loaded their weapons onto the wagon, and Benfield drove the wagon back toward the staging lot with his own saddle bronc and those of the robbers tied behind the wagon.

Back at the staging lot, they found Wilhelmina Little had wagons positioned as Addison had instructed. She also had the men, all of them from both groups, digging latrines. "We don't want the woods around us so fouled we can't walk in them," she'd said, according to Nathan.

Kerwood stopped the wagon filled with provisions in front of the church tent. Addison told the churchmen to gather wood and start cooking fires. Then they were to return to their latrine digging duties. The churchmen were not going to eat. If they wouldn't fight to protect supplies that would keep their wives and children from starving, they would go hungry. The wives and children would be fed, however.

*****

Mariah sipped her coffee and gazed at her baby. Hope had her breakfast. She was happy, playing with her hands, snug in her baby basket atop the table.

Addison's ma, across from her daughter-in-law, was happy, too, with the baby's permission to be so.

Mariah used the peaceful morning for another purpose.

"I can see on your face, Mariah, that you're wondering how long Addison will be gone this time."

"Ma," Mariah said and paused, "is it okay to call you that?"

"Dearest Daughter, it is a blessing to hear that word come from you."

"I … I was praying, but not for Addison. I was praying for Hope and me. That we wouldn't have to get along without him." She glanced down at her hands, then back up at Ma again. "I thought I'd found love with Orson, but he was just using me. To satisfy his lust."

Ma stood, fetched the coffee pot from the stove, and topped off their mugs. Mariah waited until the older woman returned to her seat. "After I found out I was in the family way, every other man on earth would have scorned me, but Addison came to me. I told him I didn't love him. He told me he loved me enough for the three of us. And I can't pray for him. I pray for myself instead." Tears streamed down Mariah's face.

"But you love Addison now, don't you?"

Mariah sniffed and nodded.

"So much that you don't think you could live without him?" Ma said softly.

More sniffs. Another nod.

"You know that Jesus died to take away our sins, to save us from Hell, do you not?"

Again, a nod.

"The Son of God, died to save every man, woman, and child, whoever was and whoever will be. Do you see what a tremendous thing this is? So filled with love and compassion our minds cannot grasp the idea."

Ma waited. For the nod. Then she smiled. "After He did all that, do you think He will let you fight by yourself to earn heaven? He will not. He will help you carry your burdens and finish the work He started on the cross. Do you see that?"

Through tears, Mariah saw Ma rise, take the baby in the basket, and leave the house. Ma would walk down Main Street to the Meeting House. She was leaving her daughter-in-law time to cry, time to get those thoughts settled in her mind.

Time to wash the breakfast dishes.

*****

Early afternoon. Addison sat on a rear bench at the back of the tent. Cromwell stood and preached down at him. About allowing the men of his church to eat. But that was not going to happen. He was angry at the preacher and the men in his congregation for pushing him into a situation where he had to kill three men.

On the far side of the lot, Joshua Reedley crested the rise from the river bottom along with two wagons. Probably more of the Warren train. Addison stood and waved.

Reedley walked his horse across the staging lot and dismounted.

"Takes a half hour to load wagons and cross the river," the Holy Crusade Wagon Master said. Take the rest of the day to get the remaining Warren wagons across."

Addison introduced Reedley to Preacher Cromwell. The preacher's pinched lips released their grimacing pucker.

Cromwell said, "The Emigrant Aid Society told me you would

be our wagon master during our journey to Brotherton. I am very glad to see you, Mr. Reedley."

Cromwell complained that Addison had refused food to the men of his church.

Joshua turned to Addison. "Why?"

Addison explained and concluded with, "Because of him, I had to kill three men."

The preacher huffed, "I had nothing to do with the killing of those men. I tried to stop him from going after them."

"If I had not gone after those men, what would have happened, Mr. Reedley?"

"They'da come back. Probably with a few more of them. And this time, some of your people would have been killed. And maybe some of ours."

The preacher gripped the lapels of his light grey suit and lifted his chin. "We do not believe in violence."

"No matter what?" Reedley said.

Cromwell's chin lifted another inch. "No matter what."

"I have one question for you, Cromwell."

The preacher frowned, at the lack of the honorific, maybe.

"If we can get you to Brotherton, will your men vote to have Kansas enter the Union as a free state?"

"That's what we came here to do," Cromwell replied.

"This is how it's gonna work. We will do our best to protect you until the vote. After that, you will have to protect yourselves," Reedley said and spun on his heel and started to walk away.

"Wait, Mr. Wagon Master. What about this young man," he hooked a thumb at Addison, "refusing to let us eat?"

Reedley stopped, turned, and smiled. "I'm not the Wagon Master for the trip to Brotherton. He is."

Addison was surprised as all get out, but he tried to not let that show.

Cromwell looked at Addison. "What about supper?"

The just-appointed Wagon Master shook his head. "Tomorrow morning, there will be breakfast. At five o'clock. At six, all your men will assemble with axes, saws, and hatchets. They will load onto three wagons, and they will fell trees. If they work well, they will be fed dinner."

"We have morning prayer service from eight till nine," Cromwell said.

"From now until I tell you otherwise," Wagon Master Addison J. Freeman said, "you have from five till six to eat and pray."

Cromwell sputtered, "You … you godless young murderer—"

"He is not godless," Reedley growled. "He most certainly is not a murderer. You, however, are directly responsible for placing him in a position where he had to kill three men to protect your people. You better listen to him. By the way, when our church moved across Illinois, I gave our Preacher Larrimer one minute for morning prayer."

"You give the Lord one minute a day?"

"Gave. While we were on the trail. In Brotherton now, our preacher conducts a thirty-minute prayer service every morning. You better get one thing clear in your head right quick, Cromwell. Wherever you came from back east, you ain't there anymore.

"A second thing, until the Wagon Master gets us to Brotherton, we are all in danger. And the Lord expects us to protect ourselves. Does He feed us with manna? He does not. By the sweat of our brow, we earn daily bread. Will His Angels with their fiery swords save us from the pro-slavers? They will not. The Good Lord has given us the wherewithal to defend ourselves. And that is exactly what Addison did this morning when he did your work," Reedley jabbed the man's chest with a hard finger, "for you. And killed men," another jab, "you should have killed."

"Me and my people will never kill other men!"

"If it were up to me," Reedley said. "I'd leave you here and head back to Brotherton right now."

"I'm going to talk to Mr. Dobbs!"

"The Emigrant Aid Society man will be here tomorrow with the rest of your wagons and provisions. Or you can take a horse and raft over to the Kansas side and talk to him today. I sure don't expect to get any work out of you."

Addison tipped his hat to Joshua Reedley, walked to the side of the lot, and found Wilhelmina Little sitting with her husband and son. They were eating.

"Mrs. Little, you mind if I interrupt your dinner?"

"Come. Pull up that box. Sit down. I'll fix you a plate."

"Oh, no thanks, Ma'am. I et. I just wanted to ask if you needed your Little men tomorrow."

"Nope. You got a use for 'em, they're all yours."

Addison met the hostile brown eyes of a glowering, hulking Zeke. "Why'nt chew ask me?" Phrased through a mouthful of potatoes.

"Cause you ain't the Lot Boss. Got a deal for you, though, if you're interested."

Zeke cleaned the meat off a squirrel leg bone while keeping his eyes glued onto Addison.

"I got some trees to chop down and rafts to build tomorrow. If you and Clem will help, I'll pay for your time with supplies. Deal?"

"They already is a raft," L'il Clem said.

"Right. A two-wagon-at-a-time raft. Takes forever to get a whole wagon train over. We're going to build two more four-wagon rafts. Those same rafts will serve you all when you're ready to go."

"We'll do 'er," Zeke said. "Next time, ask me direct."

"Next time, I'll do like I done this time. I'll ask the Lot Boss first."

L'il Clem started to stand. Mrs. Little snapped, "Don't!" Clem looked a little littler as sat back down.

Addison checked his pocket watch. Almost four. Below the bluff, moonlight puddled silver on the Missouri near the ferry crossing. He looked up at the half-moon hanging over … St. Louis, maybe? More likely Hannibal. He smiled remembering school back in Illinois. Mrs. Larrimer had brought a globe to class to show her students the world. She'd explained that an inch on her model of the earth represented hundreds, or even thousands of miles. Comprehending that had been a stretch for him, but he'd come to see that was exactly what his teacher had done for him that day. Stretched his mind. Helped him see the enormity of God's universe, and how tiny was the pinhole-sized spot occupied by Found Grace Church community back in northeastern Illinois.

Thank, You, Father God of heaven and earth, for teach—

"Mornin', Mr. Freeman?"

Addison spun around. A hatless man, about his own age, though difficult to say precisely in the features muddying moonlight, stood between two of the wagons with an armload of firewood.

He suppressed the annoyance he felt at allowing himself to be snuck up on by one of the eastern pilgrims. "Mornin' to you, Mr. …?"

"Milo Eddington, sir."

There was plenty of light to see the grin blossom on Milo's face. "You're going to bang those horseshoes, aren't you, Mr. Freeman?"

Addison said, "They were planning on getting up at five, weren't they?"

Milo carefully placed the firewood on the ground next to a wagon tongue. "They were … are."

"Mr. Eddington, would you care to do the honors?"

He hesitated. "Preacher Cromwell's likely to—"

"I'll do it then."

"No, no, Mr. Freeman. I'll do it. Um, if the offer's still open."

Addison handed over the iron. "Don't hold back now."

Milo whanged. With enthusiasm.

"What in tarnation?" Came from the wagon behind Addison and Milo. A moon lit hand pushed aside the drape hanging over the opening behind the driver bench. Cromwell's head poked through the opening. Wild, scraggly, ghost-hair framed his face. The face looked both hot and frosty at the same time, He reached back inside, retrieved something, opened the lid over a watch, and held it so he could read the time. "Four o'clock in the morning! You said we would eat at five!"

"I did say that," Addison said. "And we will. Did you expect God to provide breakfast? Or maybe the people from the Warren wagon train should be made to feed you?"

"Our women feed us."

"From now on, Cromwell, you will feed yourself."

"I don't know how to cook."

"You'd better learn this morning, because for lunch, you're on your own. And I better not catch anyone helping you. Now. Get some pants on and start stacking firewood between the wagons. I want a stack the same size as the one Milo made between all the wagons. If you get it done before six, you can eat breakfast."

Addison turned and walked away. Behind him, he heard Milo say, "Best hurry, Preacher. I'll help you."

Across the lot, small fires bloomed by each of the Warren wagons.

Cromwell completed his piles of firewood at fifteen before six. He took a tin plate of food from one of the church women, sat on a bench under the tent, and stuffed eggs, potatoes, and ham into his mouth. Addison thought the man did a lot more swallowing than chewing and that he did not look like much of a preacher. His white hair stuck out and up, his shirt was dirty and untucked, and his light gray pants were dark gray in front.

At five before the hour, Cromwell rose to get a second plate of food. As soon as he sat, Addison announced, "Breakfast is over. Caleb, would you lead us in the morning prayer, please? You have one minute."

Caleb Cromwell, cheeks bulging, bewildered, looked at Addison.

My fault. I made him so hungry, I drove him to gluttony.

"Bow your heads," Addison said. "Father God, Lord of heaven and earth. We thank You for Your bountiful blessings yesterday, and for restful sleep last night. We ask, Father, that You bless our labors this day, that we commend to Your purpose. We ask that You help us embark on the last leg of our journey, soon, that You watch over us and protect us from the evil pro-slavers. And, Lord, the land of Kansas is beset by a terrible drought. Anoint that land please, with blessed rain." He looked up.

"Amen," the congregation said as one.

*****

Joshua Reedley supervised the raft builders. The Little men from the Warren wagon train and the men from Addison's group felled and trimmed enough trees for one raft by noon. The women brought a kettle of stew and biscuits for dinner. After eating, Reedley set half the men to felling more trees and the other half to lashing the first raft together.

Back at the staging lot, Addison noted one—he would not call her a Cromwell Church Woman—church woman had assumed the leadership position of the women preparing dinner. Dora Young. Addison ordered Cromwell to fetch firewood, scrub plates, and to do whatever Dora Young told him to do. Crimson shot over the erstwhile preacher's pale cheeks, but he had enough sense to keep his mouth shut.

"Mrs. Young," Addison said. "Cromwell, here, will do what you tell him. But first I need him for about thirty minutes. That okay with you?"

"Of course, Mr. Freeman."

"Cromwell," Addison said. "Fetch whatever kind of guns you have. Now"

"I have no firearms of any kind. I will not touch such a tool of the devil."

"If we are on the trail, and a bear is attacking a child from our wagon train, will your principles keep you from killing the animal and saving the child?"

"I ... I—"

"Out here, in such a situation, is a gun a tool of the devil or a blessing from the Lord?"

"I ... I will not touch a gun."

"Then I will give you one saddle horse and what clothes as will fit in saddle bags. Then you will immediately leave this wagon train."

Dora Young put her hand on Addison's arm. "Please. Give our preacher another chance. This ... this is just so foreign. Not only to him, but to all of us."

Mrs. Young. A couple of years younger than Ma. Or maybe Dora lived the same number but easier years than Ma did. But both women had their feet planted as firmly on practicality as on the ground. What she said, about this life out west being so foreign, brought to mind his own introduction to the harsh reality that existed no more than a few miles from Found Grace Church. In a place called Thompson Township. Just a couple of days into their Holy Crusade, he'd shot and killed three men. Joshua Reedley had helped Addison see the survival of the Crusade had depended on him killing those men.

"Mr. Freeman," Dora's voice brought Addison back to here and now. "Teach me to shoot. And the rest of the women."

"Yes, Ma'am. I will." He turned. "Cromwell, killing other men weighs heavy on people's souls. Some of your people will need the help of their preacher to handle that burden. Right now, you ain't no preacher. You ain't even a man. But you need to be, and you need to start becoming a man right now. If you can do that, you might figure out how to be a preacher again to these people who look to you."

"Preacher," Dora said. There was entreaty in her voice.

Cromwell hung his head and said to the toes of his boots, "I'll shoot."

Addison thought about Pa. Before Preacher Larrimer launched the Holy Crusade, his father had been the deacon in Found Grace Church. He was respected, or perhaps the position he occupied was respected. As soon as the wagon train hit the trail, though, he didn't seem capable of adjusting to the new world the congregation encountered no more than a day away from their isolated and comfortable settlement. Cromwell, too, struggled to adjust. But, was he perhaps not as inflexible as Pa had been?

On the northeastern corner of the lot, Addison gave Dora Young and Cromwell a basic lesson in handling muskets, long guns, and handguns. Then he demonstrated aiming and firing each weapon at a tree. Bark flew off the target at each round. How to load each firearm came next. Then he had Dora fire at the tree with the long gun. The tree bark remained intact. Mrs. Young reloaded and fired again. This time, bark flew.

Cromwell reloaded three times before he scored a hit. "I had to picture that bear of yours in that tree, Mr. Freeman, about to snatch one of our children before I could really aim that weapon. The first times I fired, I pictured a man there and I couldn't—"

"A bear is a simple animal, Cromwell. It's hungry. It figures we'd be good to eat. The pro-slavers, you know what they'd do to the women before they killed and scalped them. Look at me, Cromwell. You know, don't you?"

The man knew.

"And they'd kill the children and scalp them, too. Then they'd sell those scalps to those who hate us for wanting men, women, and children freed from being treated like beasts of burden."

"The Emigrant Aid Society people never told us it'd be like this," Cromwell said.

Dora said, "They told us how important it was for us to come and vote. Mr. Freeman is saying the same thing. The good Lord moved us to come here to fight this evil of slavery."

Dora was moving the man, Addison could see, more than his own words would.

The Wagon Master said, "Being able to shoot out here is a matter of life or death. Being able to shoot straight is also a matter of life or death. If you don't hit what you are shooting at with the first shot, it could give a bear or a pro-slaver the opening it or he needs to kill you. You two fire ten more rounds each. And Cromwell, you picture the devil at the end of your gunsights when you shoot."

Cromwell nodded, and Addison smiled a smile that didn't show on his face.

*****

At mid-afternoon, the Emigrant Aid Society man, Mr. Dobbs, showed up at the Missouri side staging lot. He rode a saddle bronc and brought no wagons with him. In Atchison, the wagon builder had stopped production because the drought in Kansas had stopped west bound wagon trains for the time being. Mr. Dobbs had paid the builder a premium price to produce twenty more wagons. Ziggy Hostetler also wanted more wagons. The bad news was it could take two more weeks.

Addison knew how much Mariah hated for him to be gone. Now, the separation would drag on. He wrote a long letter to his wife. Jibway Jim took mail to Brotherton. He returned with six letters from Mariah.

Over the next week, Addison used the time to push his wagon train into an on-the-trail routine. Four o'clock horseshoes. No more communal meals in the tent. Now, each family cooked their own meals over a small fire. There was daily shooting practice for everyone over the age of twelve. He appointed Dora Young to lead the morning, midday, and evening prayers. The six families with a wagon slept in or under them. The remaining eight families slept under the tent with bedding on a ground cloth.

During the day, Addison kept a crew felling and trimming logs. These were then floated across the river and moved by wagon to the sawmill. The logs provided a bit of income to augment the Emigrant Aid Society funds. Hunting parties also brought game back to the staging lot.

Ten days after arriving at the Missouri side lot, Addison asked Joshua Reedley to cross the river and see if he could figure out how much longer it would take to get their wagons. That day also, The Emigrant Aid Society man found a source for draft animals from a Mormon settlement in Missouri, north and east of the staging lot. These animals would be delivered the next day.

Joshua Reedley returned with six of the eight wagons the train needed. The remaining families would have to cram aboard the available transport and get their own conveyances on the other side. Reedley reported that Hostetler's wagons were also finished. Ziggy proposed that they gaggle up in two days' time just west of Atchison. Water would remain the critical element for their journey to Brotherton. Ziggy was bringing four water wagons with his group.

The next morning, Addison asked Mister Cromwell if he'd like to lead the morning prayer.

"Does Dora mind?"

"I asked her, and she does not."

"I'd like that. But I'll ask Dora to say the noon prayer."

At noon, Dora thanked the Lord for the delivery of fine healthy wagon pullers.

At evening prayer, Mister Cromwell prayed for rain, for an end to the drought.

Early the next morning, Addison bid farewell to the Little family. Then, his wagon train started crossing the river on two new and one old raft. After two hours, the entire train had crossed and was moving west.

Just after noon, they arrived where Ziggy waited on a dusty, dry field west of Atchison, Kansas. The bound-for-Brotherton pilgrims fed their animals hay purchased from local farmers by the Emigrant

Aid Society. Then, the pilgrims took ownership of their additional wagons and sorted out the loads.

That evening, Mister Cromwell stood in front of the driver's bench of his wagon and spent one minute praying again for rain. After which, Mr. Dobbs took his leave to return east to form up another group of free-state voters.

At the same time, Ziggy hey-upped his team and set them off on their nighttime journey toward Brotherton and the setting sun, which hid behind a wall of dark cloud. Ziggy drove the lead wagon with half his others behind him. Then came Addison's twenty. Ziggy's other wagons caboose-d the combined train.

Nightfall. It did seem as if darkness had suddenly fallen on them. Ahead, the sky remained dark. Overhead and behind, however, stars studded the heavens.

Addison assigned Dora Young to drive the first wagon of his train. Her husband Eli rode a saddle bronc next to her, and Addison rode next to Eli.

Addison said, "Mr. Young, you remind me of Joshua Reedley. Before we set out on our Holy Crusade, we all judged Mr. Reedley to be quiet, unassuming, wouldn't say 'Ow!' if you stomped on his toe. But two days into our trip to Kansas, we were a disorganized rabble and hard-pressed to make five miles a day. Then Preacher Larrimer made Joshua wagon master. We made twenty miles that day and more the next. Now all of us from Brotherton know him to be a man who sees a thing that needs doing, and done right now, and he does it. Right now."

They rode along for a couple of clip clops, and Eli Young said, "Why you telling me this, Mr. Freeman?"

"Because," Dora Young called over the rattles, squeaks, and jangles, "he thinks you might be like Mr. Reedley, and he's trying to figure out if he's right."

"Huh," Eli said. "I don't know nothing about being a wagon master."

"We'll teach you that."

To the west, the sky was still unbroken darkness. In the starlight from directly above, Addison could not see even a hint of a face under Mr. Young's hat. The hat seemed suspended on a ghost head about two hands above his shoulders. The Wagon Master could feel the man thinking, though.

Young said, "I'll do whatever you and Reedley tell me."

"That's not what I want from you, Mr. Young. I want you to see what needs doing and to get it done because you know it needs doing, not because Reedley or me tell you to do it."

They rode along then, in silence, because there was more to think about than to talk about.

Ziggy Hostetler stopped the train when he judged the animals needed rest, fodder, and water. At the second stop, Ziggy came up to Addison, who was unsaddling Outlaw. "Addison, gotta say. I'm surprised. Your train is keeping up gist fine. I'd heard they was lucky-to-make-half-a-dozen-miles-a-day pilgrims. What'd you do to fire 'em up?"

"He didn't feed them unless they worked for their supper." Reedley walked up from behind Addison. He added, "Jibway just rode in. He wants us to see a pro-slaver he caught."

A lit lantern burned a hole in the night from atop the driver bench of Hostetler's wagon. A young man sat on the ground and leaned against a front wheel. He wore face hair that was trying to be whiskers and had blood on his left sleeve. The arm was in a sling.

As he, Reedley, Eli Young, and Hostetler approached, Addison noticed Jibway did not take his eyes off the seated man.

"Where'd you catch him?" Ziggy said.

"By Willow Creek. He was asleep south of the ford. Horse smelled him. I snuck up and woke him. He came at me with a knife. I wounded him. So's he could talk."

"He tell you anything?" Reedley said.

Jibway kicked the sole of the young man's boot. "Tell him."

"We planned to spring an ambush when you got to Willow Creek. We thought it'd take longer fer y'all to git there, though, saddled as you was with pilgrims and all."

"How many of you was gonna bushwhack us, Fuzz Face?" Ziggy said.

No answer. Jibway kicked his sole again. "Answer the man's questions, or I'll start kicking you where it hurts."

"Twenty. Or thereabouts."

"Twenty," Ziggy said. "What's your name, Fuzz Face?"

No answer. Jibway moved beside the seated man and drew back his boot to kick him.

"Bill Young," Fuzz Face said.

Addison glanced at Eli Young to see if there was a reaction to the bushwhacker's name. But Eli's face showed nothing.

Ziggy said, "Git him up off his butt."

Jibway grabbed the young man's good arm and jerked him upright and away from the wagon.

Ziggy climbed onto the wheel, reached under the driver bench, pulled out a ledger book, and stepped down. Holding the book up to the light. He'd turn a page, slide his finger from top to bottom on one side, then do the same on the other. On the third page, Ziggy stopped.

"Young. First name Bill. I paroled you ten months ago, halfway between Willow Creek and Pott's Trading Post." Ziggy shook his head. "You bushwhackers. Don't know why I bother with paroles for you ... you—"

"Forked-tongue devil liars," Jibway offered.

"Mister Young, first name Bill. You want us to get the preacher?" Ziggy said.

Even in the dim lantern light, Addison saw a sudden pallor wash out Fuzz Face's tan. "You ain't gonna shoot me!?"

Addison heard a little question in the statement and even less hope.

"No preacher, then," Ziggy said. "Jibway, fetch a shovel."

"Wait. Wait. I want a preacher."

"Eli," Addison said. "Fetch Mr. Cromwell. Tell him a prisoner is about to be executed and wants to talk to a preacher. Tell Caleb he is one again."

"Hold him, Mr. Freeman. Please," Jibway said to Addison.

Addison took the parole breaker's good arm. He spied a smirk curl the lips of his blood brother. *Mr. Freeman. In honor of me being Wagon Master, probably.*

Eli and Caleb Cromwell returned, as did Jibway, with two shovels and a pick. Caleb walked up to Addison.

"This is the one to be executed?" the preacher said.

"Yes."

A small smile of compassion softened Cromwell's face. "What's he done?"

"Broke parole?"

"Broke parole. What does that mean?"

Addison explained.

"That right, young man?" The smile of compassion gone now. "You gave your parole and then broke your word?"

"Uh, Preacher, can we talk? Off to the side? Just you and me?"

Addison shook his head.

Cromwell thought about it a moment; then said, "Young man, there is not much time. You should spend it getting right with God. Put all other considerations out of your mind. Are you sorry for breaking your solemn promise?"

"Preacher. If I kin gist talk to you alone—"

Cromwell dropped to his knees and lifted his head and arms to the stars above. "Father God of heaven and earth. Break this poor sinner's heart of stone. Free his eyes from the scales that blind him. Help him to repent. Help him to accept your grace and forgiveness. Amen."

Cromwell, a preacher once more, rose, turned his back on the sinner, and walked away.

"No. No. Wait," the prisoner bleated.

Ziggy grabbed the lantern, took the prisoner's arm from Addison, and half led, half dragged the young man twenty feet across the road to where Jibway and Eli Young were climbing out of a waist-deep grave. Ziggy shoved the parole breaker into the hole. When the condemned man hit the bottom, he screamed and rolled over. His eyes were big in the lantern light. They stayed open wide after Joshua Reedley shot him.

Reedley and Ziggy walked away. Addison told Jibway he and Eli would close the grave. By the time the first shovelful of dirt clumped onto the parole breaker, the Indian's starlit ghost image was crossing the road.

Eli said, "I was afraid you were going to ask me to shoot him. I didn't want to shoot someone with my last name."

Addison said, "I was afraid Reedley would ask me to shoot him. Right then, I didn't want to shoot someone with any last name."

*****

Addison stuck the shovels and the pick in the back of Hostetler's wagon. "Eli," he said. "Can you talk to the people of our wagon train, tell them what happened and why it had to happen?"

In front, two of Ziggy's men harnessed a fresh team.

"You only got a couple of minutes," Addison said.

"I'll get the horseshoes," Eli said. "You put them in our wagon for this purpose, didn't you?"

"I can't see the future, Mr. Young. But I wanted them to be there in case the right opportunity came along."

Ziggy's wagon sat beside the road. The others were all circled up with the extra animals in the center.

Eli Young retrieved the whanging shoes and climbed up in front of the driver's bench. He whanged the shoes.

The people, including Preacher Cromwell, gathered in front of Eli. He said, in a voice just short of hollering. "One of our scouts captured a pro-slaver who was set on ambushing us. Turns out this man had tried to bushwhack Mr. Hostetler once before. Ziggy showed the young man mercy. If the man promised to never bear arms against him again, Ziggy would let him go. The man promised, and he was released. Now, ten months later, here was this same man. He intended to ambush Mr. Hostetler a second time. We shot the man and buried him. Notice I said we shot him. One man pulled the trigger, but we all shot him. He busted his solemn promise, and if we had let him go a second time, odds are he would have tried to attack us again. He was a sheepdog that developed a taste for mutton. Now we'll be pulling out shortly. Preacher Cromwell. Would you lead us in prayer? You got one minute."

Addison took his hat off.

The preacher stayed on the ground. He removed his hat. "Lord of heaven and earth. Help all of us pilgrims to accept this hard new land. Help us hang onto the purity in our souls. Help us do the hard things this 'Bloody Kansas' pushes us to do without sinning to do them. And Father, please bless this parched land with blessed rain. Amen."

A flash of lightning split the sky to the west. Thunder crashed and settled into a menacing grumble. Horses screamed and whinnied. Children just screamed.

Preacher Cromwell, you need to be careful what you pray for!

A big splop of ice-cold water splatted on Addison's head.

He put his hat back on.

Drops pitter-pattered on the brim for a moment; then the clouds seemed to bust open and dump months of stored-up rain in an instant. Except the deluge kept coming. Whipping winds drove sheets of water sideways from one direction, then another.

Addison stood next to Eli Young and was about to tell the older man what to do, when Eli shouted to his wife Dora, "Get the women and children into the wagons. Tell the women to drive from inside the wagon cover."

Then Eli grabbed one of the men from Preacher Cromwell's church by the arm—Solomon Wurtz—and told him to have the men round up the cows and extra horses and tether them to the wagons.

Addison hollered, "Wait. Get your slickers on first. Then take care of the animals."

"We're already soaked," Eli said.

"The slickers will help you keep some body heat. Otherwise, you'll chill so bad you can't do nothing but shiver. Slickers first. Then tend the animals."

The extinguished cooking fires hissed. The chimney on the lamp next to Eli Young shattered, and the wick fire snuffed. All Addison's blinded eyes saw was profound blackness rent down the middle by the remembered flash of lightning. His eyes, ever so slowly, began to adjust. At the moment, the dark seemed impenetrable. And most likely full of pro-slavers ready to spring their deadly ambush.

"Jibway Jim," Addison shouted. "Joshua Reedley."

"I'm here," Reedley said from his right. "I told Jibway to return to Willow Creek, ride two miles south, then turn east. See if he runs into those bushwhackers that … parole breaker mentioned."

"We need more scouts. How about we pair up one of our experienced guys with a pilgrim?"

Reedley agreed and hustled off to find his men.

Lanterns blinked on inside a few of the covered wagons, like fireflies so scared they couldn't blink off.

Addison found Eli Young. "Round up four good men. Have them meet me at Hostetler's wagon. Have 'em bring saddle horses."

A lantern glowed through the cover of Ziggy's Conestoga. Walking toward that glow, Addison's boots splashed puddled water but didn't sink in mud. Yet. Once they got to moving, though, forty sets of wheels would churn the prairie into a swamp.

As he strode forward, the wind died. Thank You, God, for that blessing.

Reedley stood next to Ziggy and Charlie McTavish, one of the men Joshua'd brought along to scout for the journey to and from Atchison.

"Charlie," Reedley said, "round up the other scouts. Don't take more than five minutes, though. Then come back even if you don't find any of them."

Ziggy climbed up onto his wagon. "Joshua, Addison, I'm pushing off. I've told my drivers to drive out on the prairie. We'll let the Pilgrim Church folks have the road. But have them split into two lines. One line for each side of the road. Hopefully, we will not churn up so much mud someone gets stuck. We're heading off now. Get your pilgrims moving quick as you can."

Ziggy snapped his bull whip over the ears of his mules, and his wagon lurched forward. The rest of his train pulled out of the circle and spread out onto the prairie.

"Ziggy's got riders out front on both sides of the road. Are they scouts?" Addison said.

"Sort of," Reedley replied. They're scouting for prairie dog towns, not bushwhackers."

Addison nodded. Though it was too dark for Reedley to see it. But it made sense. Mules with busted legs and wagons with broken wheels would mean more trouble than the rain.

Joshua Reedley and Eli Young paired up scout teams and deployed them to the front and rear of the Conestogas. Eli walked away. Addison said to Joshua, "Won't take forty days and nights of Preacher Cromwell's deluge to float our Prairie Schooners."

Reedley humphed and said, "Wiseacre!"

Before the Holy Crusade began, the people of Found Grace Church had called Joshua's son Maurice the Wiseacre.

Reedley announced he was scouting to the southeast of the road. If the bushwhackers came after them, that's where they were likely to come from.

"Want me to ride with you?" Addison said.

"Stay with your train, Wagon Master."

Wagon Master and former Wagon Master entered the circle of Conestogas, where everyone and everything seemed to be in motion. Some of Ziggy's schooners pulled out of the circle and headed west. Pilgrim men harnessed teams and tethered animals. And all the while, God continued to bless them abundantly with what Preacher Cromwell had prayed for.

Addison and Eli Young moved among the Pilgrim wagons, encouraging, suggesting, threatening, and growling. Pilgrim wagons started moving. Each had a lantern glowing from inside. Except for one of Ziggy's, which was filled with gunpowder and shot.

Once they had the entire train moving, Addison asked Eli, "You want to ride in front or in back of our train?"

"Back. That's where we're most likely to have trouble."

If it hadn't been so dark, Addison would have had to work hard to keep his smile from showing. Eli had chosen what Addison himself would have chosen if Joshua Reedley had asked him where he wanted to ride.

With the dark, the hard cold rain, and nothing to do but bob along on Outlaw, the journey settled into an endurance contest. There was nothing to see but the lantern glow from a couple of wagons in front of him. Hooves splop, splopped. Trace chains jangled. Rain drummed on his hat brim and spattered on his shoulders. The monotonous sound joined the other discomfits in a mind-numbing assault on Addison's attentiveness. Even though he was soaked and cold, there was an enticing thought that he could just close his eyes, and he would sleep through the ordeal. And it wouldn't even matter if Outlaw kept them up with the train.

A violent shiver shook Addison awake. *Did I sleep an instant or an hour?*

Being Wagon Master in daylight and warmth was one thing. This was entirely different.

When the wall of weather had moved over them, the temperature dropped considerably. His slicker kept him from getting wetter, but he'd been soaked before he donned it. And it did not prevent the chill from slithering frosty fingers beneath it to touch skin trying to preserve any vestige of warmth.

Another shiver, smaller this time, shuddered through him. Ahead, beyond the three glowing lanterns all he could see was the blackest black night God had ever inflicted on the earth. Addison had the sense, the fear, that he and Outlaw and all the wagons would suddenly fall, that Ziggy had led them off the end of the world.

In the wagon next to him and Outlaw, Dora Young spoke to her team. "That's it, you beautiful beasts of burden. One hoof in front of the other. Just keep it up. We'd be just as miserable if we stopped. So, keep going. When we do stop, you'll get the biggest bag of oats you ever et." Then she'd start over with the same words again.

Addison thought of speaking to Outlaw, but the will to do so ran up against rocks of mindless plodding along. For a moment. Then it sank in. He was Wagon Master, and he was allowing Dora

Young to do his job. Normally, Addison worked to keep his mind on his job and not on Mariah and Hope. That morning, however, he needed something to keep his brain working instead of wallowing in self-pity over the ugly conditions.

"I was just thinking, Outlaw," Addison said. "About how much Mariah and Hope mean to me. Maybe we should get us a mare. Ma's two buggy horses being stallions, too."

Outlaw continued to splop along, his head hung down a bit.

From the lead wagon, Dora was into the "one hoof in front of the other" part of her spiel.

"Nothing to add to the conversation here, Outlaw?"

The horse shook its head from side to side.

"You know, Outlaw," I'm reminded of St. Paul's letter to the Corinthians, one of them anyway. The one where he talks about faith, hope, and love. And the greatest being love. If the saint were here right now, I wonder if he would think hope, at this time, in this place, is the greatest?"

"I sure do," Dora said. "I hope there will be a morning to end this dreadful, everlasting night. I hope we can cross Willow Creek and not have to wait in mud up to our axles for it to subside."

"Ah! Mrs. Young," Addison said. "Do you see it? Directly ahead. The sky is a lighter shade of black."

"Sometimes, young Mister Freeman, too much hope will color a man's perception."

"Huh. Well, youthful Mrs. Young, my hat is keeping the rain out of my eyes, and I can tell directly ahead of us, the blackness is lighter than to the sides."

Dora Young said, "Lord of heaven, Lord of earth, thank You for blessing our Pilgrim Wagon Train with a Wagon Master whose body has eyes as perceptive as the hope-filled eyes of his soul."

"You see it, too, Mrs. Young?"

"No, but I hope you are seeing it right and true."

Outlaw snorted.

Wagon Master, time to check on your train.

Addison wheeled Outlaw around, cut behind Dora's wagon, and

pulled even with the one on the left side of the road. He raised his voice above the rain. "Who's driving?"

"Samantha Ewald." The voice came out strong from under the canvas.

"You holding up, Ma'am?"

"Course I'm holdin' up. Got a dry, sittin' down job. Wish I could rig some sort of slickers for the team, though. If I did rig something, the wind'd probably come up and blow it away."

"Sun'll be up before too long, Ma'am."

"Great! Then we can see how miserable we are."

Addison didn't know how to get out of the conversation gracefully. Or any other way.

"Thanks for cheering me up, Wagon Master."

"Ma'am." Addison tipped his hat.

He nudged his horse to move next to the wagon following Dora's. Outlaw bobbed its head up and down.

"You laughing at me?"

The horse bobbed his head again.

The reins ran under the canvas cover, and it felt strange, not being able to see who … to whom he was speaking.

He repeated his question about holding up.

"Yep."

The men and older children were out on the prairie, mounted, leading the extra horses and cows. They had to learn how to function in bad conditions. These pilgrim women, however, he'd expected them to be beat down, demoralized by the weather. As he moved to the other side of the road, the invisible driver greeted him with, "I'm already cheerful as I can be, Wagon Master."

A wagon train of wiseacres, that's what I got!

Addison stopped Outlaw. The wagons splashed ahead to either side of him. The women drivers flicked the reins occasionally, and occasionally, they said, "Hey up."

"Outlaw. I thought I'd give these women hope. Instead, they gave us some. I see you ain't hanging your head anymore."

His mount snorted.

The last of his Conestogas passed. Eli Young, on foot and leading his horse by the reins stopped beside Addison.

"We're churning up the edges of the road pretty good," Eli said. "I think we should spread our wagons out onto the prairie, like Ziggy did."

"Good idea. The middle of the road, though, is in great shape. Ride forward and tell Dora to drive down the center. Then spread the following wagons out. And you can have our last wagon drive down the middle, also."

Eli mounted and rode forward. Addison rode aft and talked to Ziggy's man, Godfrey Mason. The last of Hostetler's wagons traveled over churned up prairie. All these teams were working hard.

"Be good to stop and put fresh mules to work," Godfrey said. "Be good to have a cup of coffee, too. Right now, I'd trade all four of our water wagons for two sticks of dry firewood."

"You carry firewood, don't you?"

"Yeah. All Ziggy's drivers carry it. If we forgot to pack some, Hostetler would take his bullwhip to us. It's just that when you want coffee bad and cain't have it, why, bellyaching turns out to be the next best thing. And if it's a good bellyache, it don't have to make sense."

Rain continued to fall. The teams slogged along.

"Them Pilgrims," Godfrey said. "Bet they don't got no firewood."

"Our—Addison had almost said 'my'—pilgrims have fire makings in each wagon."

"Well, I'll be. Pilgrims with trail sense!"

Back on the Missouri side staging lot, Addison hadn't called the daily lessons he held for the Cromwell Church People "trail sense lessons." Rather, he'd called them 'what you gotta know to get there' learnin'." He told his pupils, "Folks call the state next door 'Bleeding Kansas.' That ain't its only nickname. 'Hard to cross' is another."

Each morning session began with: "One. Don't waste time. The quicker we get to Brotherton, the quicker you become safe and comfortable. Two. Everybody over the age of ten works. Three. Take care of the animals. We can't get there without them. And this is Number Zero. Because it comes before Number One. Always have a gun to hand. But, and this is even more important, don't shoot another church person."

Outlaw shook his head and brought his rider back to the west side of the Missouri River. The rain, not quite so heavy now. Ahead, black. Maybe not quite so black.

"I'll ride ahead and talk to Ziggy," Addison told Godfrey.

Outlaw moved them forward. Addison spoke to each woman driver as he passed. "We'll stop soon." "Hang on a little longer." "Be sunup soon."

"Sure hope so," one said.

Before he passed Dora Young's wagon, he retrieved the whanging horseshoes and rode on. When he caught up to Hostetler, he reported how hard the draft animals were working in the rear of the train.

"Time to stop," Ziggy said, "I'll fire my pistol."

"Save your powder. I have the horseshoes."

"Whang 'em then."

Addison whanged them. The signal to circle the wagons: two gunshots or the horseshoes.

Ziggy moved his wagon to the right, off the road, and stopped. His drivers began to form the circle.

When Dora drove her wagon past, he said, "Look east, Mrs. Young. It's gray."

"Look west, Mr. Freeman. It's gray there too."

"I'll put my hope in the rising sun," Addison said.

"I'll put my hope in the dark sky in the west growing lighter. Kansas needed the rain. Now we need it to stop."

Be nice to get in the last word with that woman. Just once.

Eli Young rode up beside the wagon master and laughed. "I know what you're thinking."

As soon as the circle formed, some of Ziggy's men rigged canvas shelters from the sides of two wagons. Wash tubs were placed under the canvas awnings and filled with wood. Tinder fires flared up, ebbed a bit, then the kindling caught and threw off light that was as welcome as the warmth.

Eli and Dora Young directed the pilgrims to do the same thing:

build two shelters and two fires. Those who were not working on that task, filled feed bags for the horses and mules and put out hay for the cows.

Just outside the circle, Addison and Eli dug latrine pits. Beneath a couple of inches of the mud, the earth was still a hard crust. Once they busted through that, the digging was easier. And, though the rail still fell, and a chill rivulet snuck down the back of Addison's shirt, it was warming work. By the time they finished, the smell of coffee and bacon welcomed them back inside the circle.

Addison handed his shovel to Eli and shouted, "Preacher Cromwell. Morning prayer, please."

The preacher strode to a point between the two pilgrim cookfire awnings and removed his hat. "You men, keep your hats on." He raised his arms and lifted his face to the sky. "Lord of Heaven, Lord of Earth, thank You for blessing this parched land with this lifegiving, lifesaving water."

As the preacher prayed, water streamed down his face like his hair was crying. Addison counted off seconds. When he reached "forty-five," the preacher said, "Lord, enable us to continue our journey, and arrive safely and speedily to Brotherton. Amen."

The Church and Ziggy people echoed "Amen."

Then Ziggy hollered, "Git the kids in the wagons. We'll bring them their breakfast." And he showed his men, and the preacher's, how to use a hat to shield the plate from the rain.

It had been raining hard before. Now it rained soft. Addison noted the sky to the west was a lighter shade of gray than it was to the east. Hard rain still fell there, he figured.

After the women and children had been fed, Ziggy loaded a plate for himself and stood next to Addison under the cooking-fire tent. For a time, Hostetler ate as if starved. He held his tin plate close to his mouth and in front of his chin whiskers. His lips smacked, and he grunted as he forked in potatoes and egg and chewed with bulging cheeks. After mopping his plate clean with a half-eaten biscuit, he belched and wiped his whiskers with the back of a hand.

The awning sagged with puddled rain. Dora Young took a stick, warned those standing near the edge of covering, lifted the center, and spilled the water. Then she took Ziggy's empty plate and handed him a steaming cup of coffee.

"Thankee kindly," Hostetler said. "Your husband about?"

"You want to talk to him?"

"Yes. I'm going to offer him four mules for you."

"He'll tell you I'm worth eight mules, and if you buy me, I'll tell you the chewing tobacco and the whiskers have to go. Another thing. You give Eli all those mules, I will not wear a harness and pull a wagon for you. Just so you know."

It was crowded under the cooking awning. And quiet, as the men and women looked at Ziggy to see if he had anything else to say. Dora, too, waited, it seemed, for him to respond. When she walked away, it started: guffaws and, "Gotcha you good, din't she;" "That Dora;" "Bet you don't never yank her chain agin."

The laughter rose, peaked, and ebbed. Addison looked up at the cookfire awning. Quiet. The thrumming of the rain had ceased. Next to him, Ziggy said, "Fine coffee." He drained his tin cup. "Mighty fine coffee." Then he said, "I figure we keep the train here for a day. Give the prairie time to dry out a bit."

Hostetler picked a man to ride with him to check the condition of the road and on Willow Creek. Before the two departed, Ziggy said to Addison, "Bushwhackers."

Rats! Shouldn't need to be reminded to keep some part of my mind on them all the time.

Addison paired lookout teams from the young men and young women and deployed them to posts a mile to the east both north and south of the road. Two additional pairs were sent west. They were to maintain those posts until relieved or until they spotted anyone approaching. Then one of the lookouts would ride to the train and inform the wagon master.

Eli Young and Godfrey Mason would be in charge. Addison told them, "Together you serve as wagon master. Singular. Can you handle that?"

They said they could. Godfrey asked, "You goin' someplace?"

"Yeah. I'm going to take Charlie McTavish and ride toward Leavenworth. If pro-slavers come after us, that's most likely where they'll come from."

The animals had befouled the ground inside the circle of wagons. Addison told Eli and Godfrey to move and reestablish the circle to the west a few yards, but to leave the horses and cows where they were, hobbled and inside a rope corral.

"Pick six men and/or women who can shoot as a response team if the lookouts spot something. Keep six horses saddled for them."

Eli and Godfrey nodded.

"Everyone," Addison said. "stays on their toes. Everyone stays armed. You two take turns sleeping. One of you needs to be awake all the time. Have the people sleep in shifts too. If Charlie and me ain't back by sundown, move the animals back inside the circle."

Eli and Godfrey stared, like two robins in a nest of four chicks wondering if they'd get a bit of worm next.

"Questions?"

"No, Sir," in a two-person singular response to the Wagon Master.

9

As they rode toward the rising sun, Addison checked on Charlie McTavish frequently. Charlie was fifty yards behind. Where Jibway would be if he were there.

"Tail-end Charlie's where he's supposed to be," he reported to Outlaw.

The horse snorted.

"Keep my mind on the business at hand, that what you mean?" Outlaw bobbed his head.

Addison squinted, as much to clench his brain muscles as to protect against the eye- burning sunlight. He was tired enough to lay down in the mud, without spreading the ground cloth, and sleep all day. But he couldn't do that. He had to determine if bushwhackers were coming.

Ahead, nothing but unbroken prairie. He made a tsk, tsk. His mount set into a canter. Addison looked back. Charlie's horse had kicked it up, too.

If he'd been with Jibway, he and his blood brother would have taken turns riding in front. The McTavish kid was all right, but he wasn't Jibway. His blood brother had powers of observation Addison would never have. Still, he trusted his own exhaustion-state perception more than Charlie's wide-awake powers.

Addison checked the position of the sun. About eleven. He could have pulled his pocket watch, but that seemed like too much effort.

Ahead, shimmering in the heat, a hazy image began to take shape. A copse of small trees. An oasis of the prairie. They were headed right for it. It could be shelter for Charlie and him. It could be a great ambush spot for bushwhackers. The wind was from behind him, so Outlaw couldn't smell other horses, if any were there. He swung to the right, intending to pass to the south of the saplings.

When the stand of trees was well behind them, Addison checked his watch. 12:30. Time was important. He wanted to cover as much ground in the direction of the threat and then rejoin the wagon train before it crossed Willow Creek. But he was dead tired. He reined up, stepped down onto wobbly legs, and waved Charlie to join him.

Addison unsaddled Outlaw, rubbed his back with the saddle blanket, and looped a rope around his neck.

The McTavish kid rode up, dismounted, and yawned prodigiously.

"Charlie, I gotta grab some shuteye. Wake me after two hours. You can sleep then."

The kid had spent half the night asleep in the back of a wagon.

Addison spread his ground cloth and placed the saddle on it. He looked up at Charlie as he yawned again. "You think you should sleep first?"

"Um. No. No, sir."

Addison took the end of Outlaw's neck-rope and tied it to his wrist. Then he lay down on the ground cloth.

"Outlaw, if McTavish falls asleep, bite his ear off."

"I won't sleep."

Addison rolled onto his side so the kid couldn't see him smile. He placed his hat over the side of his head. Mariah flitted through his thoughts. Then Hope did. Then, in the place where thinking happened, it turned dark.

*****

At church service Friday morning, Mariah sat at the center aisle end of the back pew. Preacher Larrimer had not positioned himself behind the podium yet. It was quiet in the church. Except for the lullaby patter of rain on the roof. Usually, the preacher didn't dally with morning prayer. Usually, he kicked off the service promptly, prayed efficiently, and sent the men and women off to tend fields or to build Brotherton. That morning, the pause dragged on. Next to her on the pew, Sean O'Riley smelled of his wet Irish wolfhound.

The preacher, in his stern black suit, moved to his podium, and raised his eyes to heaven. He began with, "Listen, brothers and sisters. Listen to the holy music the rain is making for our service this morning. Thank You, God, for this blessed rain." He went on to say that the drought had brought home to him how much people depended on God for salvation and survival. "Salvation," he thundered, "as grace-filled people, we should always carry salvation first in our minds, in our hearts, and in our souls."

The preacher gripped the sides of his podium, hung his head, and allowed a pause to develop. Except for the rain, it was quiet. Hear a pin-drop quiet. Addison had told her when Larrimer did something like this, it was prelude to him really cutting loose. This pause, too, dragged on.

The preacher looked up, and said, "I confess to you, my brothers and sisters, that I sinned. I became overly concerned with the drought. I did not trust the Lord to ensure our survival. And, so, I let salvation slip from my fingers."

Mariah was astounded. Preacher Larrimer, man of God. A blameless, sinless rock of moral rectitude. He was for her, a pillar of cloud by day and pillar of fire by night, showing the straight and narrow way to grace and salvation.

Outside, wind gusted and drove the rain splattering against the side of the church, driving away the peaceful sound of it pattering on the roof.

"I ask you, my brothers and sisters," said in a subdued, throaty rumble, "to forgive me."

Forgive Preacher Larrimer! Was that possible? Would God allow such a thing?

Mariah raised her hand to her mouth. Some of the ladies seated in front of her raised hands to mouths or over their hearts. A weighty cloud seemed to fill the church, preventing anyone from speaking.

But then, Orson Seiling stood. "Preacher, in all of New Found Grace Church, I'm the biggest sinner you got. Whatever forgiveness I got in me, it's all yours."

After bowing to his forgiver, the forgiven raised his hands to the congregation in supplication.

Agatha Jansen rose from her seat and moved to the deacon podium.

Addison had told Mariah about Agatha. At the start of the Holy Crusade, Deacon Sylvan Waverly had been left in charge of the stay-behind members of Found Grace Church while the other half of the congregation traveled to Kansas. The deacon was to sell the property of the Crusaders and forward the money to them in Kansas. Then, when summoned, he was to lead the remainder of the people to Kansas to reunite Found Grace Church. Instead, he seized the property of the Crusaders and distributed it among the stay-behinds.

Word of Waverly's treachery reached the wagon train, and Joshua Reedley and Addison traveled back to Found Grace Church. There, they captured Waverly and looked for another man to take charge of the stay-behinds, but they considered none of males trustworthy. Stay-behind women put forward Agatha Jansen's name. Reedley trusted her and left her in charge. It turned out to be a good decision. After Addison's father had been removed from the deacon position, Agatha was appointed. A woman deacon. Unimaginable. Until it happened.

Now, when everyone in New Found Grace Church appeared afraid to speak, Agatha spoke. "Preacher Larrimer, we need you to forgive my brothers and sisters and me for not jumping to our feet and giving you what you asked for. Your confession surprised us, though. Plumb knocked the stuffing out of me."

Outside, the wind whistled around the church and the rain slapped against the windows.

Then Agatha said, "Preacher Larrimer, we forgive you.."

She invited her brothers and sisters to say the words together. They became her echo.

Outside, the wind died down, and the rain resumed its soothing patter on the roof.

The preacher thanked his congregation, cleared his throat, and, from that point on, conducted a normal prayer service. The hymns and prayers went on for a while. Mariah was not anxious for it to end. No one else seemed to want that either. Then Sean O'Riley's stomach growled.

Preacher Larrimer didn't smile often, but he did then and concluded the service. His congregation belted out a lusty and holy "Amen!"

Mariah stayed seated as everyone else filed out to go next door to the Meeting House. She played over again the entire prayer service and resolved to write down her recollections that afternoon. She wanted to be able to share the experience with Addison.

Father, watch over him, please. Her prayer every time her husband came to mind.

*****

Dearest Addison

Saturday evening. The supper dishes are done. Hope is sleeping in her bed. Your mother is knitting in a chair in the living room. And I am alone with you, wherever you are.

In the last letters you wrote, you were in a staging lot on the Missouri side of the river. I hope you are still there. I can't imagine how hard it would have been to bear all of yesterday's rain—yesterday's blessed rain, Preacher Larrimer reminded us often to call it such—to bear all of yesterday's blessed rain on the trail. I pray now and often that God will keep you safe.

Wherever you are.

I wrote last night about our extraordinary prayer service yesterday. We had another, just as extraordinary, this morning. Before that, though, we convened in the Meeting House. Mayor Gallant Argyl reported to us that the Territorial Legislature had thrown out the pro-slavery Lecompton Constitution that was in effect when we arrived in Brotherton. In its place, the Legislature approved the Wyandotte Constitution, which forbids slavery.

The mayor pointed out that we Free-staters had been protesting the voting fraud and irregularities for a year to get that Lecompton document overturned. The pro-slavery forces are even now yowling in protest over the Wyandotte laws. Preacher Larrimer said we had to redouble our efforts and our prayers to preserve this new constitution.

"It is what the Lord had us come here to do," he said. "Our votes helped overturn the old constitution. Our prayers will preserve the new one."

We reconvened in the church at eight. Preacher Larrimer was in fine fettle. His voice rattled the windows, as you would say, as he called on God to keep His helping hand fixed on our efforts to abolish the abomination of slavery.

At this moment I feel so blessed. Well, as blessed as I can be when you are not here. But blessed because we had a small part in moving Kansas toward free statehood. Blessed because of Hope and your mother and the people of Brotherton. And because of you. And because I feel like I am with you.

Wherever you

Hope fussed from the bedroom.
"I'll see to her," Mrs. Freeman said.
"I think she wants to nurse." Mariah laid down her pen.

*****

Addison woke, though his eyes remained closed. His lips twitched into a tiny smile. He reached out for Mariah and … grabbed a handful of mud.

Just then, his horse tugged the rope tight around his left wrist. He sat up. Outlaw stared intently to the southeast. His ears cocked forward.

Behind Addison, Charlie lay on his ground cover, asleep with his head on his saddle.

Addison wiped his hand on his pants, freed the rope from his left hand, and grabbed Charlie's shirt, and jerked him upright.

"Someone's coming," Addison said. "Get your horse down. Lay across his neck. Talk to it, so he stays quiet."

"Sorry," Charlie said all, sheepish like.

Addison slapped Charlie on the cheek. "Time for sorry later. Get your horse down. Now! And take the hobble off."

They both had their mounts lying down in the tall grass. Charlie talked soft baby talk. Addison listened. Outlaw twitched his up ear.

"Addison J. Freeman," came a shout. "Reedley and I are coming in."

Jibway Jim! It was funny. Jibway, an Ojibway Indian, spoke better English than most of the white folks in Kansas.

Addison stood. Outlaw worked himself to a standing position, too. Charlie and his horse followed suit.

Jibway rode up, hopped down from his big black stallion, and gripped his blood brother's arms. Reedley trailed with a string of six horses roped together.

"Look, Joshua Reedley." Jibway pointed. "Now Addison take mud brother."

Charlie rubbed his hand over his cheek. The dirty smudge stuck though.

Reedley stared, for a moment, at McTavish, then those hard eyes moved to a new target.

Addison desperately wanted to surrender victory in the stare down, but he forced his eyes to stay engaged. Joshua was not trying to win a schoolboy game; rather, he was determining if Addison measured up to being a guide and model to the McTavish kid.

I did what I had to do. What I did was the best I could do.

Reedley nodded. Addison wondered, as he had before, if Joshua could read his mind.

Jibway interjected, "What? No one liked my joke?"

Addison responded, "A joke? Is that what that was?"

"Mud brother! You no understand?" Jibway said. "Maybe I need teach you English, Blood Brother."

Addison shook his head, regretting launching into this banter with Jibway. Most of the time, his blood brother was as closed-mouthed as Joshua Reedley. Occasionally, though, he turned himself into one of those I-will-get-the-last-word-in-or-die-trying types. And he'd gone into Injun speak to boot.

Reedley switched his saddle to the first one in the string of horses.

"Where'd you get those?" Addison asked.

"Last night, I saw this campfire ahead of me. A sizeable group. I could tell that from a ways out. As I was sneaking closer, Jibway rose out of the grass and grabbed my arm. Almost peed myself."

"Not almost," from Jibway. "I smell it."

Reedley ignored the intervention and continued. "The group, they were laughing, talking. Obviously drinking. Thirteen pro-slavers,".

Jibway: "All young. Barely able to grow whiskers."

Reedley: "They weren't watching. We got close."

"They laughed about ambushing us, killing the men, and what they'd do to the women."

"Then they'd kill them, too."

Reedley tightened the cinch strap.

Jibway: "They left one sentry awake, and the rest fell asleep."

"Jibway took care of the sentry. Then we gathered up their guns and woke the drunks. One of them pulled a pistol I missed, and I shot him."

"Reedley wrote their names in a notebook—like Ziggy's— and put them on parole."

"We took their guns, boots, and horses."

Jibway: "Seven horses were branded. We turned them loose."

Reedley: "You two coming with us?" which abruptly terminated the conversation.

Addison and Charlie hustled their saddling.

"How far away is the wagon train?" Reedley asked Addison.

"We should be there around sunset."

They were.

10

Next morning, after the horseshoes whanged, Addison and Jibway grabbed quick breakfasts and set out for Willow Creek. Overhead, the black sky was unmarked by starry spots. Jibway had told him that stars were sun dust left behind when the source of daylight traveled across the sky the previous day.

"When it rains, does it wash the sun dust from the sky?" Addison had asked his blood brother.

"Course not. Sun leave dust very high in sky. Great Spirit set rain clouds closer to earth. Everybody know that."

Jibway kicked his big black into a trot. Outlaw followed.

It seemed like the longer he knew his blood brother, the more he discovered he didn't know about him. Jibway did attend Preacher Larrimer's services, but Addison wasn't sure if the civilized Indian worshipped God or the Great Spirit. Or if the Two were the same supreme being endowed with different names by different people. Addison knew to Whom he should pray, though.

Please, God, can you wait to bless us with more rain until after we get the wagons across Willow Creek?

Eli Young and five other mounted men, all with axes, followed the blood brothers. Charlie McTavish drove one of the empty water wagons.

It was midmorning when they arrived at Willow Creek. The

water level had returned to pre-drought level. The approaches to the ford were, as Ziggy had reported when he'd inspected the crossing the day before, soupy mud from the high-water-level mark down to the edge of the stream.

Addison dismounted in the middle of the road. Jibway and Addison glanced at each other. The glance said, "Goodbye."

Jibway pointed his big black south and headed down stream. After three miles, he'd turn east. Looking for pro-slavers. It would not do to have bushwhackers descend on the pilgrim wagon train as they crossed the creek. Intercepting that bunch of drunken kids and preventing them from committing their mischief and murder was fortunate, but that didn't rule out the possibility of a more adult evil enterprise being afoot.

Eli Young and his axe men reined up next to Addison.

"Eli," Addison said. "Stay with me. The rest of you go up stream and start chopping down trees. We need to build a corduroy road across the mud to the creek and up the bank on the other side." He checked to see if they all wore sidearms. They did. "If you decide to take your boots off to walk through the mud to get to the trees, okay, but do not, **do not**, take your gun belts off."

"We're going to be working in deep mud and water for a spell," Addison said. "I don't want to ruin my boots." He stood on a leg and removed one boot and sock, then stood on the bare foot and removed the other. After lashing his boots to the rolled ground cloth, he swung up onto the saddle.

Eli scooted back off his saddle, hiked his legs up, removed his boots and socks, and secured them.

Some years past, Ziggy had had his men build a rocky bottom to the crossing, Addison explained to Eli. "We need to make sure the flood didn't wash the rocks away." The water in the stream was still muddy.

Addison headed for the stream, hugging the left edge of the road. He pointed for Eli to ride along other side. Outlaw entered the water, and it appeared the solid bottom of the ford had remained intact. Halfway across, the water came up to Outlaw's belly. The west bank of the creek sloped up gradually, so there was a sizeable stretch of soupy mud to cross on that side, too.

"We need a lot of logs laid down," Eli remarked.

Addison didn't answer. He turned Outlaw, and they recrossed the stream as Charlie McTavish stopped his water wagon in the road short of the high-water mark.

"Pull the wagon off the road," Addison told Charlie. Then he and Eli took the lengths of lumber, wedged against the sides of the water barrel to hold it in place, and placed the boards so they'd serve as a slide for moving the big water tank to the ground. They used ropes secured to saddle horns to haul the barrel off the wagon. With that task done, Addison directed Charlie to haul chopped-down trees to the crossing.

*****

The wagon train arrived at the crossing at three that afternoon. The corduroy road was completed on the eastern shore of Willow Creek but only half done on the other side.

Addison was barefoot and lashing a supporting sapling along the side and top of the corduroy road on the western side. He stood straight, looked at the train of wagons, then up at the sky covered over with black, rain-swollen clouds.

"Keep the men working," Addison said to Eli Young. "I'm going to talk to Ziggy and Joshua Reedley. I think we need to start moving wagons across even though the road isn't completely done on this side."

Addison swung onto the saddle and crossed the stream. Ziggy, as usual, drove the lead wagon. Reedley was out scouting, but Ziggy, after looking at the sky, agreed.

He said, "Hey up, mules."

Addison and two of Hostetler's mounted men hustled through the mud beside the corduroy and crossed the stream ahead of Ziggy. Once the wagon reached the end of the sapling-covered road on the west side, Addison had the two riders string their lariats to the wagon to assist the mules pulling it through the last few feet of soupy mud.

After the first six wagons crossed, the water wagon brought a piled high load of saplings to the crossing. Ziggy wanted to continue crossing the way they were. Addison disagreed. He halted the wagons while the corduroy was completed.

"Your boys work fast," Ziggy said.

Two dozen men, from both Hostetler's crew and the pilgrims, laid logs and secured them in place. Addison was just about to wave the next wagon across when Joshua Reedley rode up to the work party from the north. He reined up next to the just finished section of corduroy and eyed the men. They were all barefoot, standing in ankle deep mud, wearing mud-spattered clothes and mud-smeared faces.

"Addison J. Freeman," Reedley said. "A man with many, many mud brothers."

A sudden quiet settled over the crossing, to be broken by a thunder of laughter.

Fortunately, the sky remained silent. Until the last pilgrim wagon crossed the ford and rumbled across the saplings and joined the circle of wagons.

Then there was sky thunder. And rain.

*****

Mariah Freeman sat in her office in the Meeting House writing notes in her patient ledger. A knock on the frame of the open door paused her pen.

"Miz Freeman, you got a minute?"

Mariah smiled at Maybell Jim. "Of course. Come in."

She was Jibway Jim's wife. The roster of Brotherton residents included OJibway Jim. But, of course, everyone called him Jibway. As to his last name, Mayor Gallant Argyl said Jim was a perfectly good first name and equally good as a last. Thus, Maybell Jim.

She is Colored popped into Mariah's mind. The thought triggered automatically, but once it did, she pushed it aside. Preacher often said, "We are all God's creatures, and He created us equal." She believed that with all her heart, but she also knew believing didn't necessarily make it easy to practice a thing. Where she had grown up in the middle of Illinois, Colored people had a status equal to pets and farm animals who could speak. She resolved anew to work harder at living up to Preacher's words.

Mariah pointed to a chair. Maybell sat.

"Are you feeling ill, Maybell?"

"No'um. Not here for healin. Like to ask a question. If'n dats all right?"

"Of course."

"Do Addison write you letters?" Maybell fidgeted. "Is it okay I ask dat?"

"Yes, and yes. I got two letters from him last week. He hadn't started back here yet. A problem with supplies and wagons for the next wagon train of 'Pilgrims,' he called them, from the east."

"Thank you kindly, Ma'am. That's what I wanted to know. Where was they and when was they coming home?"

"First thing, Maybell, if you call me ma'am, I will have to call you Mrs. Jim. So, can you call me Mariah?"

"Yes, Mmm—. Yes, Mariah. It be hard, though. When I was young, if that ma'am didn't pop outta my mouth regular like, I got a stick taken to me. I guess those switchins' learnt me so good, it's hard to unlearn it."

Mariah took the woman's hand. "Believe me, Maybell, I know what you're talking about. By the way. Addison did say he expected they would get on the way to us soon."

"Then we have that rain. You think that slowed 'em … Mariah?"

"It was a heavy rain, and thank You, God. We sure needed it, but, yes, I would expect it delayed them. And it's raining again today. Still, hopefully, we'll see or hear from them any day now. And Maybell, from now on, when I get a letter from Addison, I'll let you know what he writes. About where they are. That sort of thing."

"Thankee kindly, Ma'am … Oops. Sorry. It gist slipped out agin."

"Tell you what, Mrs. Jim. When they get back, we'll have you two over for supper. There, we can tell them that when they leave us again, they have to write us two letters a week. They have to write it together. So, some of it is from Jibway to you, and the other is from Addison to me."

"I knowed—knew it was a good idea to come talk to you." Maybell shook her head. "And don't it just beat all? Jibway, an Injun, is trying to teach me how to speak English good!"

*****

Addison woke. To pitch darkness. And snores. He'd fallen asleep on top of supplies in one of Ziggy's wagons. Crowded in with five other men. Something was not right, though. He lay still and listened hard, trying to push his hearing beyond the log sawing.

Rain. Or rather, the lack of it. The sound of drops on the wagon canvas cover was missing. Ah, the rain stopped. As quickly as his mind offered that excuse for waking him, he rejected it. Something else had roused him. He sat up, grabbed a pistol in each hand, cocked them, and pointed one forward and the other to the rear.

"Approachin' the wagon!"

Ziggy. And his voice was loud enough to drown out whanging horseshoes.

A lantern shined in through the front opening. Two of the men with him rose onto an elbow. The other three kept snoring.

"Addison." Ziggy's growl. "Gitchure pants on."

The lantern walked away.

He lowered the hammers, set the weapons down, and pulled up his pants without bothering the guys sleeping to either side of him. Too much. They grunted and rolled away from him.

"We need to come, too?" one of the awake ones asked.

Addison pulled on his boots. "Ziggy woulda said. Go back to sleep."

He slid out of the wagon, and his boots squished mud. *Mud! More dadburned mud. How about bringing the drought back, G—.*

"Sorry, God," he mumbled as he put on his shirt. *Lord, it's as if my mind has a mind of its own. And try as I might to control it, it has a strong disposition to bellyache, bitch, bad mouth, and yes, Lord, blaspheme. Sorry.*

Confession was supposed to be good for the soul. His soul did not feel good. As a matter of fact, his soul almost hankered for Pa to take a switch to his body. He shook his head and put on his guns and hat and walked forward two wagons. There, Dora had a fire going. The smell of coffee pleased Addison's body and soul. He took the tin cup offered by Mrs. Young, sipped, and said, "God bless you, Ma'am."

She shined a "Good morning" smile at him as she returned to the fire and placed bacon slices into two skillets.

Joshua, Jibway, Ziggy, and Eli Young sat on crates under the awning over the fire, leaving the empty chair for Addison.

Reedley said, "Jibway, tell Addison."

Fatigue was written all over his blood brother's face. "South of here, I found sign of a large party, more than fifty horses. They were headed towards a spot halfway between Lawrence and Prairetown."

"Could be they're aiming to do what you warned us about, Addison," Joshua said. "Sneak around us and come at Brotherton from the west."

"Yeah," Ziggy said. "But that's gist a poss'bility. We … you cain't rule out an attack from any direction."

Reedley recounted the pro-slavery attacks on Brotherton that had occurred last year. They'd come from the south and east. And one had come from the northeast. All of them under the awning, except Dora, glanced at Jibway, because he was the main reason that last attack had been thwarted.

Jibway's chin rested on his chest. He'd dozed off. They let him be while they decided a course of action.

After they ate, Reedley and Charlie McTavish would each take a horse and a spare and ride hard for Brotherton. There, they'd ensure the lookout posts were all manned and that defenses, in general, were put on alert.

At sunup, Ziggy and Eli Young would get the wagons moving west. Depending on road conditions, it could take three days to get to the Delaware River crossing east and a little south of Brotherton.

Addison would manage the scouts around the Pilgrims. The Pilgrims was how they'd come to talk about the entire assembly of

Conestogas. Even Ziggy didn't' quibble over being included in that label.

The Pilgrims wrapped up their planning session as Dora began loading plates. Each man got an egg.

"Last of them," Dora warned.

Addison woke Jibway and asked him if he wanted to eat.

"Sleep," his blood brother replied.

"There's an egg," Dora said.

"You eat it," Jibway said. "Cooks should get some of the good grub, too."

Horseshoes whanged.

The Pilgrims rose, and the Ojibway laid down where his blood brother had been.

*****

"Slogging through this nasty mud," Ziggy said, "confuses the hell outta my mules. They think they must be pulling loads up a mountain, but when they look, all they see is pancake-flat Kansas."

The second day, the mud was not quite so deep, but the draft animals still labored as if the drivers had set the brakes on their wagons. That night, Addison sent two riders ahead to arrange for fresh teams to meet the Pilgrims.

After a third day of muddy road and prairie, men from Brotherton, with fresh teams, met up with the Pilgrims. Without those rested beasts of burden, the wagon train would have had to add a day to their journey because the horses and mules were plumb played out.

The Brotherton men brought not only fresh draft animals, they also brought news of the pro-free-state Wyandotte Constitution replacing the pro-slavery Lecompton one. The news evoked no small amount of hooting and hollering from Ziggy's men. The Pilgrims, however, responded with more restraint. Apparently, they didn't appreciate being freed from the oppressive feel that, after their Holy Crusade, after their battles along the way, after the fights for survival in Kansas, everything was still stacked in favor of the pro-slavers. But now that was changed with the Wyandotte Constitution.

The Pilgrims, Addison thought, had learned a little about Kansas. Like maybe passing through first grade, but they still had years of learning ahead of them, with the lessons growing harder and harder.

Addison pulled himself back to muddy Kanass, grinned, removed his hat, looked up at heaven, and said, "Father God of heaven and earth, thank You for the hope this new constitution brings."

"Addison," Eli Young said. "A pro-free-state constitution, I mean, I can see that's good news. But Ziggy's men make it seem like it's Christmas and Easter all rolled into one."

Addison explained how it seemed as if everything had been stacked against the free-staters, that the pro-slavers had everything in their favor, including the law. "In Brotherton, we worked hard to build ourselves a town, but if the state voted to enter the Union as a slave state, it would all have been for nothing."

11

At midafternoon, Mariah sat behind her desk, with her door closed, nursing Hope. A knocked sounded.

"Is it urgent? I'm feeding my baby."

"Our baby," came through the door.

"Addison!" Mariah jumped up. Hope lost the nipple and started waving her free arm and frowning. Mama got baby attached again before she fussed.

Addison opened the door and stood there. His eyes danced from baby to mother, baby to mother. Then he went to her. Holding Hope in place with one arm, Mariah put her other arm on her husband's shoulder, and she kissed him, neither perfunctorily nor shallowly.

He pulled back, and his eyes brimmed with matrimonial and parental affection.

"Mariah, as Hope draws life from you for her body and her soul, so I draw life from you for my soul and body."

Then they kissed again.

Without disturbing Hope.

The clanging of the church bell next door, though, disturbed the heck out of the infant. It also dumped cold water onto their kiss. A few of the babies out in the opposite corner of the Meeting Room did not like the bell, either.

"Sweetheart," Mariah said. "You want to go out and see what's going on?"

"No. I just got here. I'll wait until you finish with Hope. Then we'll go together."

"We are only half finished. Go. No matter what it is, surely, we'll have tonight together."

*****

Addison's eyes did not want to let go of the scene: wife, mother, infant daughter. The three of them blended into a … trinity. He was reluctant to let his mind use holy trinity. Then, his mind argued: If the sight of Mariah as two entities, wife and mother, together with their infant daughter, was not holy, it was not possible for anything on or of earth to be holy.

He saw it then. Something so beautiful could only come from God. The Holy Trinity of heaven had blessed him with a holy trinity on earth. Upper case HT for heaven, lower case for earth kept it free from sin, free from blasphemy.

"Husband, I can feel your mind muscles lifting heavy thoughts around. Don't forget them. Tell me tonight. Now go. Find out what's going on."

He sighed, forced his eyes to let go of wife, and of child. He turned, stepped through the door, and closed it.

The church bell rang again.

Addison sucked in a deep breath and sighed it out again.

Marshal David McTavish and Mayor Gallant Argyl were pulling the curtains closed to separate the Meeting House into two chambers.

"Addison," Marshal McTavish said in a voice that grabbed a man and planted his feet firmly onto a very practical earth. "I heard you were back. When were you going to report to me? Oh, never mind. I was young once, too."

The mayor and the marshal strode toward the Main Street entrance to the Meeting House, where people were filing inside. The mayor directed Marvin Dinwiddie to tell his wife Viola, principal of the school, to keep the children working at their lessons.

Whatever was going on wasn't an immediate danger to the town or its citizens. Once everyone was inside, there weren't enough chairs. Several of the men had to stand along the Main Street wall. The citizenry of Brotherton had grown to the point where slicing the Meeting House in half to serve two purposes was already not working. And the Pilgrims were coming to add to the problem.

Addison headed to the rear to join the standers, but Marshal McTavish stopped him and directed him to summon Joshua Reedley and his prisoner from the kitchen add-on to the Meeting House.

Reedley and his prisoner? The marshal offered nothing further, so he'd find out what was going on with the rest of Brotherton.

Addison entered the kitchen.

Joshua sat on a chair against the far wall. His eyes flicked up, then snapped back to stare at the young man sitting opposite him.

The door next to Reedley jerked open. Joshua whipped out a pistol, cocked it, and aimed at the intruder.

The marshal's son Charlie froze. He raised his hands. "Um, sorry. I shoulda knocked. Just wanna say the horses is took care of."

Joshua eased the hammer down and re-holstered.

Red showed through Reedley's drooping eyelids. The look on his face reminded Addison of a mule that had pulled a heavy wagon through mud all day, and at sundown, didn't have enough strength to unstick a hoof to take one more step.

"How long since you slept, Mr. Reedley?" Addison said.

Joshua didn't answer, so, Charlie did. "Coupla days. He tied me onto my saddle. I slept some. He didn't."

Addison remembered his mission. "The marshal said to bring the prisoner in."

"Up," Joshua said to his prisoner.

Reedley stood. The other man didn't, until his captor grabbed a handful of shirt, jerked him to his feet, and turned him toward the door.

The guy was about Addison's own age of twenty. Spikes of his brown hair stuck up on top of his head. His sparse, scraggly face hair looked greasy. Homespun shirt: dirty. The knees of his pants: caked with dried mud. The prisoner cradled his right hand against his chest with his left. The fingernails of the right hand were black, and a dirty big toe stuck through a hole in a filthy sock.

The last thing he noted before he stepped back into the Meeting House was the young man's face. Addison did not think of himself as a kid, but that's what this guy was. And the look he wore was of a boy who'd been caught peeking through a hole in the back of the girls' outhouse at school and suffered a make-your-butt-beet-red spanking in public.

Reedley had the kid by the upper arm and propelled him forward.

"Said his name's Ira Mudd," Charlie McTavish offered.

Addison looked at Charlie to see if he was joking.

"Honest to god," McTavish proclaimed. "That's what he said."

Reedley moved Mudd to the end of the table next to where the mayor sat. With the mayor were the marshal, Preacher Larrimer, and Deacon Agatha Janson.

The mayor rapped a hammer on a chunk of scrap lumber, called the meeting to order, and invited Joshua Reedley to report.

"Mr. Mayor, ladies and gents, coupla days back, we, Charlie and Addison and me, were with the wagon train bringing people from the east to join us. Jibway Jim had been scouting to the south of the road between here and Atchison. He came across tracks of a large party of riders. More than fifty, he figured.

"As you know, we," Joshua nodded toward Charlie, "rode ahead of the wagon train to warn you all. Then we headed south, looking for Jibway's band of pro-slavers. That's what we figured them for. And we figured right.

"We found them two nights ago, west of Lawrence. They had made camp and hunkered down in the rain. We snuck up on where they had their horses, some picketed, some in a rope corral. Ira," a thumb jerk targeted the kid, "watched the animals through closed eyelids."

Charlie cut in. "We tied and gagged Mr. Mudd. Then, we counted the horses. Fifty-five. We picked six of the best ones to ride back here as our own mounts was played out. Once we'd switched saddles, we stampeded the rest of the remuda and hightailed it away from the camp."

Charlie glanced at Joshua, then continued, "We stopped sometime yesterday and questioned Mr. Mudd. He was reluctant to say anything. For a while." Another glance at Joshua. "But we persuaded him to talk. Finally, he fessed up. That gaggle of men is all pro-slavery. They planned to get well to the west of our town before they come at us. They plan to kill as many of us as they can and burn Brotherton to the ground."

"That right, Mr. Mudd?" Marshal McTavish inquired.

Mudd sat there, mute, and unmoving.

Joshua punched the kid on the shoulder, and he nodded.

"Please note in the record, Mrs. Freeman," the marshal said, "that the prisoner nodded."

Addison's ma stood behind the deacon podium from church in a rear corner of the Meeting House. She looked up at her son, briefly; then dipped her quill in ink and returned to her scribe duty.

"What happened to your hand, Mr. Mudd?" asked Agatha Janson.

"I broke his trigger finger," Reedley replied.

Agatha frowned. "You broke it?"

"I didn't have time to beat it out of him, so I broke the bone. He told us what we needed to know. His gang is all pro-slavers, and they are coming to kill us. And they are going to come at us just like Charlie told it. From the west. Just like Addison warned us."

Every eye in the place jumped to Addison. His armpits dampened some.

"Back to Mr. Mudd," Preacher Larrimer said. "And to Mr. Reedley."

Just like that, all those eyes, as suddenly as they'd lit on him, for the duration of a lightning bug flash, jumped to new targets. The sudden shift in emotions, so soon after leaving Mariah and Hope, disoriented Addison.

"I had the same first thought about the breaking of the finger as Deacon Janson." Larrimer's voice grumbled like far-off thunder. "Breaking the bone in Mr. Mudd's hand was worse than killing him." The preacher shook his head. "That of course is not true. Life is the most precious gift from God. And alongside that is salvation. What Joshua did, at first, seemed reprehensible. I now see it in a clearer light."

Larrimer squared his shoulders. "There is no 'Thou shalt not break your neighbor's finger.' Still, there is a matter of concern here. When we left Illinois, I thought we were embarking on a Holy Crusade to make of Kansas a new Holy Land. What we found along the way, and here, though, is, in the words of Mariah Freeman, a Holey Land, a place full of bullet holes. Brotherton sits in the middle of a harsh and brutal land populated with many who hate us and would do us harm. To save ourselves from slaughter, several citizens of Brotherton have had to take lives. My concern here is that the harsh measures we have had to take to save ourselves not turn us into the same sort of evil men we say we are defending ourselves from."

Addison was about to intervene when Sylvan Waverly rose from his chair.

Sylvan Waverly! The last person Addison expected to speak up in such a gathering. Since Joshua Reedley brought him back into fold, so to speak, Waverly had barely uttered a peep.

"Preacher , Deacon Janson, brothers and sisters, when Joshua Reedley returned to Found Grace Church to confront me and my sin of treachery, he announced his intention to hang me. And I thought I deserved to be hung. But Joshua said the first order of business was to select a new deacon. He picked Agatha. By the time that was done, I was able to see my sin of greed for what it was. I repented, and I believe Reedley could see that grace had returned to my soul. He let me live."

Waverly looked at his hands and raised them. "Since I arrived here at Brotherton, I have kept my mouth shut and used my hands to serve New Found Grace Church. But now I must speak. Joshua Reedley is a good man. Maybe it takes a sinner like me to see just how good he is. Maybe you all are too holy to see it."

Waverly lowered his hands. "I repeat, Joshua Reedley is a good man, and there is something we seem to have forgotten. A band of men is on the way to kill us and burn down what we have built. That's what we should be concerned with."

Hear-a-pin-drop silence filled the Meeting House. For a tick and a tock. Then, a boot scraped across a floorboard. A child whispered, "Mama." Followed by "Shhh!"

Preacher Larrimer cleared his throat and looked at Mayor Argyl.

The mayor said, "Joshua Reedley, what should we do?"

"The wagon train will arrive here this afternoon," Joshua said. "Jibway Jim is with them. Tomorrow morning, first light, Jibway and Addison should find out where the band of pro-slavers is. They need to warn us when to expect the attack."

A bang sounded inside the room.

Addison's hand shot for his gun, but it had just been Mariah. She'd dropped her patient ledger book to the floor.

12

At the end of the session in the Meeting House, Addison and Mariah returned home. He removed his boots outside the door. Inside, he took a bath. Mariah gathered his clothes and deposited them next to his boots on the side porch.

When Addison finished in the tub, he dressed for bed. Hope was down for a nap. He'd just unbuttoned the top two buttons in the back of Mariah's dress when there was a knock. He pulled on clean pants and answered the door.

Hilda Grossman, one of the original stay-behind crusaders and mother of Frieda affianced to Charlie McTavish, stood on the porch. She wore a dark gray bonnet over her light gray hair. A medium gray dress. From under which the toes of black shoes peeked.

Back in Illinois, when Addison was still in school, Joshua Reedley's son, Maurice the wiseacre, called Hilda Grossman "Happy Hilda." According to Maurice, Hilda always, just always, wore a happy face.

Now, Hilda's dark beady eyes hit Addison like a slap. Then her eyes scanned him down and back up again. She shook her head.

Addison blushed. It was just past noon. He wore nothing over his undershirt. He was barefoot.

"The first pilgrim wagons arrived," Hilda reported. "They got a man who stepped on a pointy stick. 'When he was workin' barefoot,' they said. I guess these eastern pilgrims get confused. You wear boots outside and take them off before coming inside. Anyway, the foot's infected. The mayor wants Mariah to take care of the man."

Addison frowned and shook his head.

"She ain't coming? What'll I tell the mayor?"

"She'll be there. Uh, when she's done feeding the baby."

Hilda spun on her heel and headed back to the Meeting House. Addison closed the door.

Thou shalt not make false excuses. Sorry, God.

In the bedroom, Mariah sat on the bed. She'd just removed her stockings. When he told her about the message, she started putting them back on again.

"Wait. I told her you were nursing Hope. Couldn't we—"

"Later," she said.

He said, "Rat snot!" pulled off his pants, and climbed into bed. "When I wake up, I'm taking a razor and cutting 'later' out of our dictionary."

Mariah smiled, picked up the dress she'd draped over the back of a chair, and stepped into it. "Addison, button me in back, please?"

He gave no answer.

"Asleep already," she mumbled. "Rat snot! You never sleep through me unbuttoning it."

She left the bedroom and returned a moment later. He opened an eye. She was about to lift Hope from the cradle and place her in the infant basket.

"I'll take care of her," he said.

"Addison John Freeman—" She lowered her voice to a whisper. "That was like something Orson would have done."

"Sorry," he whispered, too. "It's just that when I'm away from you, Mariah Welch Freeman, I miss you so very much, and when I see you again, my heart fills with so much love, it feels like it's about to bust apart. I should have buttoned your dress for you. Forgive me. For acting like another Orson."

Orson. She'd been amazed that Addison had forgiven her for getting pregnant by that self-centered, didn't take anything seriously, soulless, mental juvenile. She'd also been amazed that he'd forgiven

Orson himself. Mariah found it hard to forgive the aggravating man. She'd tried, she told her husband.

He told her that Orson's mother asked Reedley to take her son and help him grow up. Joshua passed the job to Addison. "Orson would not listen to me," her husband said. "So, I'd tell him something, and if he didn't respond, I'd hit him. He never fought back, just took the beating. When I was ready to give up on him, he started listening to me. So, I stopped hitting him."

Addison had taken her hands in his before continuing. "God forgave the sins of all of mankind through the Crucifixion. Maybe we should find it in our hearts to forgive this one, aggravating though he is, man."

Just then, Mariah did forgive Orson. A burden she didn't know she carried lifted from her. Addison John Freeman. There were so many reasons to love him, but even he managed to need forgiveness now and then.

Mariah said, "I'll forgive you for not buttoning me—" A hint of mischief shone out of her eyes and rode on her words. "—if you confess your sin on Deacon Agatha's Penance Pew."

The Penance Pew. Agatha Janson had created the confessional at the start of the Holy Crusade when Reedley and Addison had returned to the Found Grace Church community, deposed Deacon Waverly, and appointed Agatha to the position. One of her first acts required Reedley and Addison to sit on the Penance Pew and admit to their sin of wearing their guns inside the church.

Thinking about sitting on that bench and confessing his lust and refusal to button his wife's dress, when what he wanted, as much as he wanted air to breathe, was— he perspired.

Mariah giggled. "I forgive you, Husband. Without the public confession."

She came to the bed, leaned over, kissed him hard on the mouth for an instant, then stepped back out of his reach.

"Later," she said, left the bedroom, and then the front door closed softly behind her.

A sigh came all the way up from his toenails, and he rolled onto his side.

Ma's voice came out of his mind closet. "Each night, thank God for the blessings he bestowed on you today. If you but take a moment to look, you will see them."

He took the moment.

Thank You, Father, for sending Your Son to pay the price for forgiving all our sins. And for showing us sinful humans how to forgive.

He pondered on that a moment.

Mariah forgave me for my childish snit in refusing to button her dress, and I forgave her for "later." It is good to be Christian and believe that all sins are forgivable.

Except for pro-slavers' sin of breaking parole.

That thought jolted him out of the warm and comfortable place into which he'd been settling.

Father God, can we deal with that one later, please?

*****

An aroma of joy and happiness filled Addison and Mariah Freeman's kitchen. His ma sat at the table with them. She smiled constantly, except when forking food into her mouth and chewing. Hope, in her basket, sat on the table and gurgled and cooed, delighted with her plaything hands.

Mariah and Ma chittered like sparrows who'd just discovered spilled grain beneath their tree.

The atmosphere infected Addison, and he smiled. The picture of Mariah coming home after tending to her patient and saying, "Your ma's coming for supper. We have to hurry."

And, now, after that, and after supper, and with coffee after dessert, with the dearest beings on all of God's earth there with him, he sat snug as an unhatched butterfly cocooned from Bleeding, Holey Kansas.

Ma said, "Mariah dear, why don't you give the baby her supper.

Addison and I will do the dishes. Then, Hope will come home with me. I'll bring her back when she wakes up."

*****

Before sunrise, Addison and Jibway rode west out of Brotherton with Charlie McTavish and Orson Seiling. At noon, Jibway selected a good lookout spot for Charlie and Orson. Their instructions were: "The minute you see a large group of riders approaching, hightail it back and ring the church bell."

After eating, Addison and Jibway continued riding west until sundown. Then they made camp.

The next morning, the first thing Addison did before opening his eyes was to reach for Mariah. Revelations of the most unpleasant sort flashed one after the other like heat lightning sparking silently in the distance. Not in bed. Head on a saddle. Mariah's not here but a full day's ride away.

Then Jibway's voice—he'd had the last watch—rude and full of remonstrance: "Jibway say, Blood Brother half Injun. Now Jibway say, Mud Brother five percent Injun."

"Five percent?"

"Five. Real Injun, real warrior, leave squaw in village. Not bring along on warpath."

"Huh." Addison pulled on a boot. "When I was on watch, I heard you call Maybell's name."

Sparks flashed from a flint.

"Wind's from the south," Jibway explained in an all-business tone of voice.

The pro-slavers wouldn't be able to smell the smoke, and the stand of saplings that the prairie sprouted every now and then would shield the fire somewhat.

"The bushwhackers are back to the east," Jibway said.

Addison didn't ask how his blood brother knew that.

Jibway continued, "What we … I should have done is take Orson with me and left you with Charlie back there. Maybe it's me who's only five percent Indian."

As they sipped coffee and ate bacon and biscuits, they talked about the gang's most likely plan on how to attack Brotherton. Addison saw what Jibway was doing. The Indian was almost sure he figured out how the attack would come, but he wanted to get his blood brother's thoughts before they committed to a new course of action.

Originally, they decided, the bushwhackers intended to get well west of Brotherton and come at their target from that direction. The land they'd cross was unsettled, and the pro-slavers wouldn't expect to encounter a wagon train. None had headed west since the beginning of the drought.

"And," Addison said. "It's going to rain. Probably not today, but tomorrow. The best cover for the attack would be out of a rainy night."

"Jibway say, blood brother now forty-five percent Injun."

Addison didn't respond.

Jibway dumped the dregs of the coffee from his tin cup. "This is what we're going to do. I'll ride back to Charlie and Orson and warn them. My horse is faster than Outlaw. You clean up here, then head for Lawrence." Jibway showed Addison on the crude map they had. "I think you'll cross their trail about here."

"And I can attack them from behind."

"No, Addison. Even if they couldn't round up all the horses Reedley scattered, there'll still be more than forty of them. Don't attack them. See if you can bother them and slow them down. And, Blood Brother, don't do anything white-man stupid."

*****

Mariah left her bedroom carrying a freshly diapered, fed, and burped baby. Addison's ma had already lit a lamp in the kitchen, and she stood next to the stove."

Mrs. Freeman strode to her daughter-in-law, embraced her, and smiled grandmotherly love all over the infant. Then, she stepped back and bowed her head, "Dearest Father, thank You for the blessing of this morning." Ma's eyes lifted to caress the mother and infant. "Please watch over our son, husband, and Daddy."

"And," Mariah added, "While Addison is keeping us safe, please, Lord, keep him safe."

Ma said, "Amen," and returned to the stove and cracked eggs into a skillet.

As Mariah placed Hope in her basket on the table, she realized she hadn't prayed for Jibway and Charlie. Or Orson.

Please, Lord, watch over Jibway and Charlie. And Maybell and Frieda.

She hadn't prayed for Orson since she found out she was pregnant. The prayer then was that he'd marry her. A tiny smile raised the corners of her lips. Preacher Larrimer said, quite often, "Pray always. Your Father in heaven hears you and answers. Sometimes it isn't exactly what you prayed for, but He always answers your prayers with what is best for you."

Addison was … is what's best. Mariah placed a finger in the baby's open hand, and Hope clutched it. Firmly. Then, the baby's blue eyes looked right into her mother's soul. Addison is what is best for us, she finished the thought. And she wondered how long it had been since she'd thought of herself as I or me?

Addison is what's best for us, but why, then, is he gone all the time?

Hope frowned, and Mariah wondered if the little one was mimicking the frown that must occupy her own face. But then the smell of bacon was overpowered and banished from the kitchen. Hope had soiled her diaper. Again. Already.

Ma Freeman placed two plates on the table. "You eat. I'll take care of the little stinker."

*****

Addison found the trail of the pro-slavery gang late that afternoon. He studied the tracks they'd left. A large bunch of gaggled-together horses' hooves had churned a straight path across the prairie aimed at about where Jibway had posted Charlie and Orson.

His blood brother hadn't said what he'd do when he reached them, but Addison expected him to prod the two lookouts into an Indian level of vigilance. Then Jibway would strike south looking for—

The enemy army.

He hadn't looked at it that way before, like they were engaged in a war.

Each of the last year's attacks against the people of Brotherton had been thwarted, and afterward, there'd been a feeling that Maybe now they'll leave us alone. But the pro-slavers kept coming back. As intent on the extermination of their enemy, as the anti-slavery people were determined to survive.

Outlaw tossed his head and jerked Addison out of heavy thinking.

When Mariah arrived at church for the morning prayer service, she found Maybell waiting for her. They entered together and took seats halfway back from the front row of chairs.

Preacher Larrimer stepped behind his podium and read from Scripture as he usually did. When he began his sermon, however, he did not mention the reading but said, "I invited Preacher Cromwell to conduct the morning prayer service with me. He refused."

Mariah saw every head in front of her turn to look at the man seated in the front row who'd refused their preacher.

Larrimer smiled. Preacher Larrimer smiled? A lot of people who never smiled were grumps, mused Mariah. Like the Grossman woman. The preacher, though, wasn't a crab. He just seemed to have too many heavy concerns to have any time left for frivolity.

"Preacher Cromwell told me," Larrimer said, "he wanted his congregation to get a clean view of me, without him getting in the way. He went on to say, 'Besides, I am new here. Fresh off the boat, so to speak, having come here on a Prairie Schooner.'"

Mariah was surprised. Her husband had told her that, at first, the Pilgrim's preacher was a lot like Addison's pa. Rigid, strict, stern. Cromwell had begun to change, though it was still too early to tell what he'd changed into. Now, she was prepared to like the man, and she hadn't heard him utter a peep yet.

Another surprise lay in the fact that Brotherton expected another pro-slavery attack, and the two preachers were making jokes.

Preacher Larrimer then repeated a line from the Scripture he'd read. In two short sentences, he stated the relevance of those particular words of God to everyone in the church. He concluded with a prayer, entreating the Lord to protect them from yet another attack by the forces of pro-slavery. He then invited Mayor Gallant Argyl to address the congregation.

The heels of the mayor's boots clomped as he strode from his front-row seat to the deacon podium on the left side of the altar.

"As the preacher said, we expect another attack from the anti-free-state people of Missouri and eastern Kansas," Argyl said. "This time, though, we think they will come at us from the west. We have scouts out to confirm this."

Maybell, seated next to her, gripped Mariah's hand.

"But," the mayor continued, "The attack could come from any direction. So, we will have lookout posts manned all around Brotherton. Those assignments are listed in the Meeting House."

The mayor gripped the lapels of his coat. "We also have our normal work to do. The drought diminished our crops, but there is still enough in our fields to help us through the winter. The Emigrant Aid Society has promised us supplies, but we must do what we can for ourselves."

Argyl's blue eyes swept left to right and back again. "Those working in the fields today, have your guns with you at all times."

The mayor's hands dropped from his lapels. With his right forefinger, he tapped the podium twice. "Those building houses for our new neighbors, have your guns with you."

Tap, tap. "Those teaching in the school, have your guns with you." Tap, tap. "Those tending the young ones, have your guns with you."

After a pause, "Preachers Larrimer and Cromwell, as soon as we leave church, strap on your sidearms and keep them near to hand until we return to church this evening."

Gallant Argyl placed his hands on the sides of the podium. "One last thing. Marshall McTavish and Joshua Reedley will conduct firearms training for everyone over twelve. They will come to where you are working for this training. Otto Vogelsang will train his group of builders."

The mayor nodded to Preacher Larrimer and returned to his seat.

Larrimer said, "Reverend Cromwell, would you please lead us in a closing prayer?"

Cromwell rose to his feet. "Father in heaven, thank You for bringing us safely to Brotherton, where these holy people have built a holy place to live in the midst of hate and violence. Please bless the people of Brotherton. Bless us as we strive to do Your work. Amen."

Mariah and Maybell filed out of church with the rest of the worshipers, retrieved their sidearms from hooks in the vestibule, and headed down C Street toward Main.

Mariah's office had been relocated into the unused bedroom in Ma Freeman's abode on Main Street. The Town Council had decided, with the population growth, they needed the entire Meeting House for their purposes. The Town Council also relocated Infant Care to the dwelling at Second and C Streets, originally the home of childless Thad and Olive Tamber. They moved to a new place on Sixth Street.

Having the healer's office and the infant care center near the Meeting House was almost as good as having them located inside, as that structure was the closest thing to a fort in Brotherton.

Mariah needed to nurse Hope. Maybell was working in the fields that day, but she wanted to see Hope first.

"I be wantin' a chile a my own somethin' fierce."

Mariah corrected, "I would like to have a child of my own."

"Dem words a yours, dey sure sounded purty, but dee words, dey was empty."

They stepped along in silence. Then Mariah offered, "Your speech is pretty, but your words are empty."

Maybell perfectly parroted her friend's sentence.

Mariah stopped and faced her friend. "Very good!"

"You want I be tawkin'—" Maybell stopped and started over. "Do you want me to talk pretty all the time? Like you do?"

"Oh, Maybell. I am so sorry. I had no right to try to correct your speech. What I want you to do is to speak how you want to speak."

"I want to talk pretty. Will you help me?"

"Of course, I'll help," Mariah said. "But only if you forgive me for being presumptuous."

"I don't know what the word means, but I forgive you anyway."

The women crossed the street to the Infant Care Center, which the citizens of Brotherton called the Baby House. Inside, Maybell picked up Hope from her cradle and cooed at the little one. At first the baby tolerated being held by someone not her mother, but not for long. Mariah took the child, and Maybell left to do her duty in the fields. The fields west of town.

After nursing Hope, she turned the baby over to a fourteen-year-old girl wearing a gun belt around her waist. Mariah, too, had a holster and pistol.

As she walked toward Main Street and her office, she recalled Preacher Larrimer's sermon about guns. "They are instruments of death. No mistake about that. But they are also tools to preserve life. The pro-slavers have it in their minds to wipe us from the face of the earth to preserve the abomination of slavery. Guns are the tools they would use to reach their goal. Guns are our tools to save our own lives and to bring this bloody Kansas into the Union as a free state. And we hope, and we pray for the day when the hooks in the vestibule of our church will be used for hats and not guns."

The preacher's words did not make the gun ride more comfortably on her hip.

At Ma's house, she found Lem Wisely waiting on a chair on the front porch. He was the one who'd stepped on a stick while working barefoot. Mariah wanted to change the dressing and make sure the infection was healing.

A gun fired from across Main Street and startled Mariah. Her hand moved to the butt of her pistol. A group of men, women, and children had gathered there. They looked toward the south. A man pointed and fired a pistol. Shooting practice.

On the front door to Ma's house, Joshua Reedley had tacked a note inviting Mariah to join the practice session as soon as she was free.

"Mr. Wisely," she said as a pistol popped again, "come inside. Let's see how your foot is doing."

Lem stood on his good leg, got his crutches under his armpits, and entered the house as Mariah held the door.

*****

Addison studied the trail left by the pro-slavers. A large number of horses spaced closely together had churned up a swath of prairie. Off to both sides, the tracks of a single horse paralleled the main group.

The bushwhackers had a rear guard posted.

"Not the way I'd do it," Addison mused out loud. "I'd be ranging out to the sides of the main trail."

He said, "Tsk, tsk."

Outlaw started moving forward, after the gang. Addison reined him to the left, angling away from the main trail. "You figure we can count on that rear guard to stay close to the main trail?" The horse bobbed his head up and down.

"Winds behind us. You won't smell them."

The horse's ears twitched forward. The ear twitch also conveyed a message: If you want to contribute to accomplishing our joint effort, you will keep your yap shut!

When he was to the side of the rear guard's tracks by four or five hundred yards, Addison reined Outlaw to head north. He tsk-ed again. The horse kicked into a trot.

Every once in a while, Addison stood in the stirrups and stared intently at where the bushwhackers would be if he caught up to them. When he sat back, he turned in the saddle and checked all around him.

After an hour, Addison walked Outlaw for a time, then trotted him again.

When the sun was low but still above the horizon, Outlaw

stopped. His ears twitched forward again. Then he bobbed his head up and down.

Addison smelled it. Smoke from a woodfire. And side meat frying. The wind that had blown from the south all day had died. Otherwise, the wind would have blown the smell away from him.

He figured the bushwhackers wanted to get something to eat before the sun went down when their fire could be seen from a long distance.

Ahead, to his right, a line of saplings meandered to the southeast. A stream. Probably even had water in it.

The pro-slavers were probably behind those trees, but he, on the other hand, rode across flat prairie with nothing but knee-high grass offering cover. The rear-guard may have already spotted me.

Jibway's parting words came to him. "Don't do anything white man stupid!"

*****

Mariah rocked Hope on her shoulder. She patted the baby and cooed, "Come on, Baby. You are such a good burper. Give us a burp. You'll feel so much better. Yes, you will."

Ma Freeman was fixing supper at the stove. She said, "Be thankful you have a daughter and not a son. When Addison started school, the other boys taught him how to manufacture belches. When his pa heard him, he took a switch to him. Of course, his pa took a switch to Addison often. Right up to when he was eighteen. Then the boy turned into a man and wouldn't take it anymore."

Ma stopped mashing potatoes and stared out the back window for a moment. When the mashing resumed, she said, "Adolph preached about hope one Sunday in church. He said, 'You know when your troubles pile up, and all you want to say is Woe is me! When you need to pray the most, you look inward toward your stored-up misery, when you should be looking out and up to the Lord. Where He waits patiently for you to ask for His help. St. Paul tells us about faith, hope, and love and that the greatest is love. I suggest you cannot truly love unless you have faith. During those times when I wallow in despair, it is hope that enables me to see past my troubles to the Father above."

Ma cleaned off the masher with a spoon. "When Adolph said that, it went absolutely quiet in church. Deacon Adolph Freeman had just confessed before the whole congregation that he was a sinful man!"

"I asked Addison about his pa," Mariah said. "He wouldn't tell me." She rocked and patted. "I have heard people here talk about him, though. What I heard, I'd never expect him to say such meaning-filled words."

"Adolph was a good man," Ma said. "Until we lost Addison's sister. Then he decided we had done something to displease God, and he turned bitter and rigid and righteous."

"But he preached about hope after that happened?" Mariah said.

Ma nodded.

Hope burped.

The women smiled.

At the table, Mariah said the before-meal prayer and appended, "Please, Lord, watch over our husbands. Keep them safe and keep them on the straight and narrow path."

"Amen."

Addison was still a considerable distance from where he figured the bushwhackers set up camp. If a lookout had spotted him, he didn't think they'd send someone to check on a lone rider. To the west, the edge of the sun kissed the rim of the world. Rather than continue on toward them in daylight, he dismounted, removed the saddle, rubbed down Outlaw's back with the saddle blanket, and resaddled. Then he spread his ground cloth and lay down with a pistol in one hand and a rope from around the horse's neck looped around the other wrist. He slept for three hours.

And woke to find the land bathed in milky, silvery moonlight from a huge harvest moon hovering above the horizon. There was no breeze, no smell of woodsmoke, no sound save that of night insects. He rose, holstered his pistol, coiled the wrist rope and secured it to the saddle, and looked toward where he thought the bushwhackers were camped.

Question one: Are they still there?

Two: The weather. Jibway thought it would rain tomorrow. Tonight, the sky is clear of clouds. Is my blood brother right about the rain? And is he right thinking the bushwhackers will use the rain as cover to attack Brotherton?

Jibway had said, "Slow them down."

He remembered something else Jibway said a few months ago:

"My father told me I should get into my enemy's head." His blood brother pursed his lips, then said, "I tell father, 'No! I bring enemy inside my head.'"

Addison remembered frowning before it came to him. "Don't think like the enemy. Become the enemy. Is that what you mean?"

His answer was a lot-of-teeth-showing grin.

Addison stood with his hand on Outlaw's neck. "The enemy?" he whispered.

The horse bobbed his head and stared at where Addison thought they were.

Question one answered.

The enemy. They would have some among them who'd been out to this section of Kansas. But, they would not know the land well, not know precisely where they were, nor would they know exactly where Brotherton was located.

Then he knew what they were thinking:

> We will continue to head north, cross the Oregon Trail, and then we will turn east and attack Brotherton from due west of the town. At midnight. And out of a heavy rain.

He was pretty sure he knew what they were thinking.

Addison shook his head to clear it. He took his bow, strung it, and pulled three arrows from his quiver. Standing on the side away from the bushwhackers, he started Outlaw at a slow walk toward where he figured the rear guard had hunkered down. There'd be two, maybe even three men at the lookout post. They'd have learned from Joshua Reedley's attack. A one-man sentry was no guard at all.

Under Outlaw's neck, Addison could see across the moon lit sea of prairie grass to the dark shadow of trees where he thought the bushwhackers had stopped, eaten, and now slept. The lookout post would be between where he was and them. He'd be close to it now.

The horse stopped, bent, bit off a mouthful of grass, raised his head, and continued to stare in the direction of the trees as he chewed. Outlaw stayed there, munching two more portions of fodder.

A man stood. About sixty, maybe seventy yards away.

The silhouette spoke. "Pete, you figure that's one a our broncs from when them damned abolitionists stampeded our corral?"

Another voice: "What I figger, Sol, is you oughta go wake up Mort."

Sol: "I ain't waking him. My ears is still blistered from the last time I woke him and wan't nothin' there. I'm gonna get that horse."

"You dumb bastard!"

A second silhouette rose from the grass. Both shadow figures carried long guns.

Addison patted Outlaw's neck and then notched an arrow.

The one he figured was Pete trailed Sol by five yards. Pete carried his rifle like he was rabbit hunting, ready to bring the weapon up and fire as soon as a hare sprung from its nest. Sol, however, cradled his in the crook of his arm.

"Good looking animal," Sol said.

"Sol, wait. I don't like—"

Addison stepped clear of Outlaw, drew back the arrow, and let fly. Pete grunted, staggered, and dropped.

Sol turned. "Pete. What's wrong?" He started hustling toward his comrade, and the second arrow hit him in the back. He went down.

Addison ran to Sol, dropped his bow, placed a knee on the man's back, grabbed a handful of hair and pulled, and slit the man's throat. Then he picked up the bow and went to Pete.

His first target lay on his back with the arrow stuck in his chest. The moonlight shone on his face. His eyes were open. "Sol. You dumb bastard." A gurgling noise escaped from Pete's throat. Then he was quiet.

Addison knelt. Pete wasn't breathing.

From the trees where the bushwhackers camped, shouts and curses crossed the distance. He returned the arrow to the quiver and hung the bow across his back. Then he picked up Pete's long gun, a repeater. Pointing the weapon at the hollering, he fired until the magazine was empty. Then he picked up Sol's musket and fired it, too.

Addison swung up onto Outlaw and ran the animal due west.

Glancing over his shoulder, five riders raced after him.

His horse flew over the prairie. Addison rode hunched over. His hat blew off, and the string chaffed his throat. He checked behind. It looked like they were pulling away from their pursuers. He eased a gentle tension into the reins. Outlaw slowed.

After ten minutes, Addison slowed a bit more. He wanted the bushwhackers thinking they'd begun to catch up. Otherwise, he feared they'd return to their camp.

He tried to put himself in the pro-slavers' minds. They'd be mad as all get out, that they, the bushwhackers, had been bushwhacked twice. They'd be angry that their scheme to attack Brotherton from the west had been discovered. They'd be beyond angry that they'd had members of their group killed, while they had yet to fire a shot at the hated abolitionists.

Rat snot!

"Slow them down," Jibway had said. Addison wondered if he might have caused them to move faster, to think speed was more important than the cover of rain and night.

A bullet thwipped past, followed by the boom of a long gun.

He hauled back on the reins, and Outlaw squatted on his haunches and skidded. Before the horse stopped, he tumbled from the saddle. As soon as he was hidden by the grass, he slipped his long gun off his back. His horse stood about fifteen yards from him, looking back at the approaching riders. Addison peeked above the grass. Three riders headed right at him, mounts at a trot. Two of them rode side-by-side. The third trailed them.

Addison moved through the grass to the right, away from the trail he'd made. When the shooting started, he didn't want bullets flying in the direction of Outlaw.

At about fifty yards from Addison, the lead riders slowed their mounts to a walk. The third man also slowed.

The fourth and fifth bushwhackers were farther back. He pictured them hunkered in the grass, holding long guns, itching to find something to shoot at, and when they did, they would rise from cover and cut loose.

First, though, there's One, Two, and Three to take care of.

Addison had crawled several yards back in the direction of the bushwhackers. He didn't think they'd suspect him of that. Besides, they would think he lay wounded where he tumbled off his horse. But they'd be wary.

The two riders approached to within fifteen yards.

"You see him?" Rearmost Rider said.

"Nope," from Forward Rider One."

"Stop," Rear Rider said. "I don't like—"

Addison left his long gun on the ground, drew his pistols, rose to his knees, and fired two rounds with each gun. Forward Riders One and Two fell sideways from their saddles, as he dove back onto his stomach. Bullets cut through the grass above him.

Staying on his belly, he eased himself in the direction of Forward Rider One. He'd moved a body length when the firing ceased.

Reloading.

Who fired at me? Was it Riders Four and Five only, or did Rearmost Rider shoot, too?

He stayed flat and continued to snake his way toward where the Forward Riders fell. After a bit, he stopped, rock still, and listened hard. Not a sound. The world was as silent as a lightning bug. He resumed slithering. Then he heard moaning and froze.

A trick?

"Rafe, Fatty. Help me. I'm hurt bad."

Hooves suddenly pounded. Addison raised up and saw Rearmost Rider galloping back toward the camp. He flopped down again. Dropping the fleeing Rearmost Rider would have been easy with his long gun, but he stayed low. Riders Four and Five had their rifles aimed at where he'd poked his head above the grass. He knew they did.

"Fatty! Don't leave me!"

The voice was laced with pain and terror. Moaning resumed.

Addison rose to his hands and knees and crawled toward the voice. First, he found a man lying on his back, not moving. A horse stood next to him. The animal shied and backed up a step as Addison neared.

"Whoa, there, horse. No need to worry about me. I'm not going to hurt you. Not me. No." He kept a steady cooing as the other Forward Rider moaned and cried.

Forward Rider One had taken a round through the temple. Addison crawled past him, cooing, and cajoling the man's mount until he was able to grab the reins. Then, with the horse shielding him, he walked toward the whimpering.

A bullet had struck Forward Rider Two in his left upper arm. The sleeve was bloody. Addison felt the arm. Forward Rider Two screamed. The bone was broken.

He disarmed the wounded man, including pulling his boots off looking for a gun or a knife, but found none. Then Addison stood behind the horse and peeked over the saddle to where he thought Riders Four and Five had hunkered down. He didn't see their horses. They must have made their mounts lie down. Rearmost Rider was still visible, still hightailing it back toward the camp.

Addison untied the rolled ground cloth from behind the saddle. Inside, he found spare pants and a shirt. He took the shirt and tied the sleeves together, fashioning a sling. Looking under the horse's neck this time, he still saw no sign of Four and Five. He knelt, lifted the moaner's head, and slipped the sling over his neck. When he lifted the busted arm, the moaner screamed loud and long. Addison laid the arm back down across the man's belly.

"Mister," Addison said. "I gotta get your arm in that sling. Otherwise, you can just stay here and die."

Horses coming fast!

He peeked above the grass. Four and Five riding hard right at him. They both had pistols in their hands. Addison flopped down, grabbed his long gun, and rolled so he'd be firing from under the horse's belly. He rose to his knees, pulled the rifle against his shoulder, aimed, and fired. His target tumbled backward out of the saddle.

The other rider's pistol popped. The horse Addison hid behind screamed, reared, and fell onto its side.

He shifted his aim and fired. The last rider hunched forward, like he might stay in the saddle. Addison levered another round into the chamber. But Rider Five fell off sideways.

Is that all of them?

All. To his mind's ear, it had sounded like Jibway's "All."

Addison stayed on his knees, taking stock. In front of him, nothing showed above the grass. Behind him, he saw Outlaw, and behind him, a ways off, another horse stood looking in his direction.

Next to him, the downed horse made a noise that was half whinny, half whimper. The injured man screamed again. The wounded animal lay across his legs.

After checking in front of himself again, and seeing nothing, Addison raised his rifle and put the wounded beast out of its misery.

The screamer lay on his back. His eye sockets were puddles of shadow. His mouth was open as if he were drinking moonlight. Then he said, "My leg!"

Addison grabbed the dead horse's head and lifted it as far as he could. "Pull your leg free," he grunted through clenched teeth.

"My leg's busted!"

"One leg ain't," Addison snarled.

The screamer screamed, "I cain't!"

He laid the horse's head down gently. Just then he had more respect for the dead horse than the live man with a broken leg and arm. The man hadn't even tried to pull himself free. Addison shook his head and went to check on Riders Four and Five.

After a dozen paces, a pistol popped and he dropped into the grass, and started crawling again.

He found Four on his back. The man reached for the pistol in his shoulder holster, but Addison took the gun away from him.

"You's white!" the bushwhacker said. "We thought you was a Injun. You killed our lookouts with arrows, and you's sneaky as a damn Injun. We thought you was torturin' Wesley. That's why Ad shot hisself. He didn't want no Injun torturing him."

The pistol pop?

"Ad?" Addison asked.

"Yeah," Four said. "Addison, but everbody calls him Ad—called him Ad."

Shot a man with my own damned name! He worked hard at not swearing, not giving in to the urge to cuss like all the others, but he'd heard once, "Sometimes won't nothin' do fer a man but a good goddamn."

Addison! Yeah, you the live one. The voice of his blood brother calling him to stop daydreaming in the middle of the night. He had two enemies close to hand. They were wounded but alive. And they were enemies.

He pulled the boots off Four and found a knife in one and a derringer in the other.

"How bad you hurt," Addison said. "Can you get up?"

"Don't much feel like gittin' up."

A trail of dark liquid oozed out the corner of Four's mouth. Tobacco juice or blood?

"Don't feel like—"

Four's head rolled to the side, and he was still.

Addison left Four and found Five. He had a chest wound, and he'd shot himself in the side of his head.

Addison took a deep breath and huffed it out. Like always happened after he killed men, thoughts tried to crowd into his mind, but he closed the door to them and returned to busted up Wesley and finished the job of getting the man's arm into the sling he'd fashioned. Wesley screamed so loud it hurt Addison's ears. But, finally, he got the job done. He left the man lying there, rose to his feet, and called Outlaw. The horse came at a gallop. He mounted, caught the other saddle bronc standing close by, and rode back to the, for the moment, silent screamer.

He put a rope around the dead horse's neck, and Outlaw pulled it clear of the man, who screamed to high heaven.

The leg was broken all right. The left one.

Addison retrieved the man's long gun, unloaded it, and swung it like an ax into the ground, busting the stock off. Then he took the spare pants he'd found earlier and cut them into strips of cloth. First, he straightened the leg; then he lashed the rifle barrel to the leg. And all the while the man screamed. With the last strip of cloth secure, Addison stood.

Wesley no longer screamed. He lay on the ground panting. Addison took the man's good right arm, pulled him up onto his good right leg, and picked the man up like a bride about to carried across a threshold.

"Lift your good leg over the saddle," Addison said.

The man did. And grunted. But didn't scream again.

Once astride, Wesley said, "Why you help me like this?"

"I figger," Addison said, "One day, we'll live together here in Kansas, and we won't be shooting at each other anymore. I figger I need to practice at how to get along with folks I used to shoot at."

15

A buzz of chatter filled the crowded Meeting House. Mariah Freeman sat next to Maybell Jim in the last row with empty chairs to either side of them. The other rows were all fully occupied.

At one p.m., Marshal McTavish growled, "Come to order!"

Sentences stopped half said, and quiet filled the place. Mariah recalled the small town in central Illinois where she grew up. Such discipline was unattainable there, but since she and her parents joined the Holy Crusade wagon train, they'd had to fight to leave Illinois, fight to enter Kansas, and fight to stay. The people of Brotherton knew when to shut up and listen.

The marshal stood next to an easel with butcher paper tacked onto it. Joshua Reedley was on the other side, with Orson Seiling next to him.

"This line," the marshal pointed to a dark line drawn across the page, "is the Oregon Trail. Over there, about where Joshua Reedley's Adam's apple is, is the Brotherton Meeting House. This circle here next to me and just south of the Trail, that's called Knob's Knoll. It's a rare rise of land above the level of the prairie. These other lines represent First through Sixth Streets."

At the nod, Orson took over. "Jibway, Charlie McTavish, Addison, and me, used that knob as a lookout spot and a rendezvous point.

Charlie and me manned the post while Jibway and Addison rode on west."

Maybell grabbed Mariah's hand and squeezed it. Mariah squeezed back shared sympathy and concern.

Reedley took over. "After riding west half a day, Addison headed south looking for the bushwhackers. Jibway headed southeast. Addison and Jibway returned to Knob's Knoll early this morning."

Mariah breathed. She hadn't realized she'd been holding her breath.

"Praise be to God," Maybell whispered.

Orson took over again. "They both figured the bushwhackers would be passing Knob's Knoll just about now. And they thought the attack on Brotherton might start about eight p.m. Jibway, Addison, and Charlie are still there on the Knob. They sent me to warn you about the attack."

The buzz of murmuring that broke out then was as if a beehive had been knocked over.

"Order!" McTavish glowered at the citizen army. "This is what we're going to do. Everyone over twelve years old will have a job. Joshua Reedley has a list with the assignments. Before we get to that, here's the general plan. The threat, as we know it, is from the west. But we have to be alert to an attack coming from the east or south as well. So, we will maintain our normal lookout posts, except instead of two persons manning each post, we will have three. And one of the three will ride back every half hour and report to the mayor and Joshua."

Reedley took over. "We will also have a patrol riding up and down the Delaware River, from the lookout spot just east of here to a mile north of Sixth Street. They will have four people assigned and will also report every half hour."

McTavish again. "I will be in charge of our defenses at the west end of town. There will be two lines of defense."

He explained the first line of defense was a set of wooden barriers fifty yards beyond the end of Brotherton's streets. If they'd dug trenches, their defenders world have been stuck in water filled ditches for hours on end, so Otto Vogelsang had the barriers built. There would also be a tarp over the area behind the barricade to keep the people at least somewhat dry. The second line would be the last house on each street. Each of these houses would have two rifle men or women, plus young weapon loaders.

The marshal went on. "I will be with the first line defenders. If we have to fall back, I will fire a flare." The marshal held up a strange-looking gun. "Got this from a riverboat man on the trip from St. Louis." McTavish smiled at the gun as if he were showing a picture of a grandson.

"Anyway," he was all business again, "If I fire a flare, us barricaders will move to here." He pointed to an extension of third street on the butcher paper drawing. "Once I fire the flare, move rapidly to this point. The extension of Third Street. Don't dawdle. As soon as everyone is assembled, I will fire another flare. That will be the signal for those in the houses to start firing. They will leave us a safe corridor along the Third Street line. Under cover of their fire, we'll be able to fall back and join the people in the houses."

Joshua Reedley conveyed instructions to the reserve force, which would wait in the Meeting House. Mayor Gallant Argyl would be stationed there as well to receive the reports from the scouting parties and confer with Joshua Reedley as to appropriate responses to threats.

Marshal McTavish then adjourned the general meeting with, "We've got a lot of work to do this afternoon. But everyone should find an opportunity to get two hours of sleep before sundown."

Mariah would be stationed in the Meeting House. Maybell, and Orson, part of the reserve force, would be there, too.

So many times on the journey to Kansas, danger came at them suddenly, with no time to think or plan. This time with all this warning, there was so much time to worry.

But there was also time to pray. That was good. Very good.

*****

From atop Knob's Knoll, Addison. Jibway, and Charlie McTavish watched for the bushwhackers. There were no trees on top of the knoll, so Jibway had posted them below the top on the south side so they would not silhouette themselves. Jibway and Charlie sat cross legged on their slickers and leaned against each other.

Addison knew Jibway could sleep like that, even in the conditions they were experiencing. He wasn't sure Charlie would be able to sleep though.

Steady rain pattered on the brim of Adison's hat. To the south, nothing moved out of the murky mist. A small stand of saplings stood off to the right, a mile away, Jibway had told him. Those trees defined the extent of visibility. Through the binoculars, Addison scanned all the way from due east to due west. Nothing. Lowering the binocs, he rubbed his eyes, then finger wiped the lenses of the binocs and flicked off the water. Scanning slowly again, starting with east, he moved the glasses as he breathed innnn and owwwt. When he faced due south, he stopped scanning. His heart thumped his chest like an inside out mea culpa.

Three mounted men sat their mounts staring at the knoll. Two of them had long glasses *aimed right at me!*

"Jibway," Addison whispered. "Three men by mile-away trees. Don't stand up."

Jibway stood up. He stared intently to the south. "Charlie, mount up. We're leaving."

"Jibway, what are you doing?" Addison said.

"You, Blood Brother, are still tender foot. Keep mouth shut, eyes open, then, by and by, you learn things."

Jibway mounted and headed his big black down the knoll and toward Brotherton. Charlie rode close behind him.

Addison checked on the three. They were only two now. Both had glasses aimed at him.

Did the other one ride back to alert the main body?

Addison ran to Outlaw, swung up onto the saddle, and started after his blood brother. Not even half down the knoll, he reined up next to Jibway and Charlie waiting by a stand of saplings.

"They come after us?" Jibway said.

"Yes," Addison said. "Only two of them, though."

"We will kill them," Jibway said. "Charlie. Hold the horses and wait here."

"Damn!" Charlie said. "I always have to hold the horses."

Jibway stared at him for a moment.

Addison sat and waited. Rain spattering on the ground joined the sound of rain peppering his hat.

Jibway faced Addison. "You hold the horses."

Addison stepped down and took the reins of Charlie's horse. Charlie grinned.

His blood brother led his mount to Addison and handed over the reins, then Jibway headed back toward the oncoming bushwhackers. Charlie fell into trail behind him.

The Indian stopped. "Get your rifle, Charlie."

"Yes, sir."

Addison wasn't mad. About being left behind. To hold the horses. No. Not mad. Exactly. More like put out some.

Addison smoothed his slicker beneath him, like a woman gathering her dress under her as she sat in church. He sat cross-legged on the muddy ground and tilted his head back a bit, not so far as to let the rain get in his eyes. The gray sky looked close enough to reach out and grab a handful of it. Of course, he didn't have to bother reaching. The sky was dropping on him drip by drip.

"Wasn't that long ago," he mumbled to Outlaw. "We had a drought, and the prairie was baked dry and hard as a rock. Now, instead of no rain, we got too much. Mud everywhere."

Outlaw lowered his head and bumped Addison on the shoulder, almost knocking him over.

"Hey, what's the matter with you!"

"Everything's the matter," Jibway said from behind him. "Stand up and look." He pointed southeast.

Addison pushed himself up. There, just at the edge of visibility, about a mile away. The band of bushwhackers.

Jibway: "Heading the way they are, they'll come onto the town more from the south than the west. I'm going to warn them. You and

Charlie tail them," he pointed at the bushwhackers, "but be careful. They've grown wily. Those two who were riding right at us stopped about half a mile away, turned, and rode back south. Must've smelled an ambush. So, you watch out they don't ambush you."

Jibway slung his long gun over his back, swung up onto the saddle, and headed down the slope paralleling the bushwhackers.

"You figger he'll get there in time?" Charlie said.

Addison nodded. "He won't be able to give our folks much of a warning, but it'll be a lot better than no warning."

"What are we going to do?"

*****

A shout woke Mariah. It took a moment to remember where she was. In the Meeting House. In her walled-off corner office. Atop blankets on the floor. The next shout, she understood. "Joshua Reedley!" And Jibway Jim did the shouting. She'd slept clothed. As she pulled on her shoes, a raised voice from out in the hall said, "Reedley's out back."

The outhouse.

Jibway said, "Maurice, get your father. Quick. Mr. Niedlinger, go and ring the church bell. Then signal attack from the south."

A general ringing signaled danger. Then a moment of bell silence was followed by one, two, three, four single clangs. One meant attack from the north. Two meant east, three south, and four was west.

Mariah's turned the knob on her lamp, and the room brightened. Then she opened the door to the hall.

At the front of the large room, men scurried to raise the wicks of the wall-mounted lamps.

Jibway shouted, "Leave those lamps the way they are. Get your guns and boots. Hustle. Mr. Fishboch, Mr. Dinwiddie, check the houses on Main Street from here to the west end of town. Make sure we have two shooters in each one."

The church bell clanged. Her heart was already beating fast. Now, it beat faster. She reentered her former office and strapped on her belt gun.

Father God, holy is Your name. Be with Addison. She lowered her head till her chin rested on her chest. Be with Hope. Be with us. Please.

In the Meeting House proper, Joshua Reedley and Marshal McTavish were forming a party to ambush the bushwhackers.

"We need six wagons." Urgency sparked in Reedley's voice. "No canvas covers over them. Load a Otto Vogelsang barricade in each one." He started pointing at men, and women, to accomplish the wagon roundup.

In front of Mariah, the pointed-at people began hurrying toward the door.

"Now," Reedley said, "I need another twenty people. Coupla' horse holders, but the rest gotta be good with firearms."

"I want to go," Mariah said.

Joshua looked at her. "Doc, I figured you'd wait back here till the shooting was done. Then we'd send for you."

"I don't want to go as a healer. I want to be behind a barricade."

*****

Addison thought the bushwhackers would use some sort of trailing-the-group rotating lookouts. One rider would stop and watch the trail for a minute; then, he'd ride to catch up while another stopped and waited for the first man to pass. He'd wait a minute then he'd ride to catch up. Something like that.

Instead of trying to attack from the rear, the better chance was to ride hard to get ahead of them a bit, pick a spot, and ambush them from the side.

"What are we going to do?" Charlie said that a lot.

Instead of answering, Addison looped the sling on his rifle over his shoulder, swung up onto Outlaw, and set him into an all-out run. The bushwhackers were riding at a gallop. It'd take a bit to get far enough ahead to pull his ambush. He didn't turn to see if Charlie followed.

The footing descending Knob's Knoll was decent. On the prairie, there were low spots with deeper mud, a danger Outlaw could sink a hoof and break a leg, so horse and man concentrated on avoiding such obstacles. He worried whether Charlie was still with him. Off to his right, though, he could just make out the dark shadowed form of the gaggle of bushwhackers. He was pulling ahead of them. That was good.

To the west, the dim light from the setting sun would still be enough to silhouette him, and Charlie. Not good.

Outlaw ran hard and eased them ahead of the pro-slavers. Mist and dark gloom hid the gaggle. Addison glanced back. Charlie was behind him. As he faced front again, the wind whipped off his hat. Hunkering low in the saddle, he got his hat back on and pulled it down tight. The hat kept the rain out his eyes.

His horse had run hard long enough. He could feel it. He eased a little pressure into the reins. Outlaw slowed, and Addison angled him toward the track the enemy followed. He did not want to be directly in front of them. Otherwise, when they came after him, he might have to ride directly for Brotherton and wind up shot by the people he was trying to protect.

When he estimated the enemy gaggle would ride past him a half mile away, he stopped, dismounted, and pulled Outlaw down and onto his side. Charlie reined up next to him.

The kid was waiting to be told what to do!

"Step down," Addison said. "Move away from me. Get your horse down. We're going to shoot at the bushwhackers, and they will shoot back. Laying down, there's less chance one of our horses will take a bullet."

"I figure we're close to the Oregon Trail. Brotherton ain't much more'n a coupla miles beyond that. We could ride there and join our folks."

"We could. You want to ride for Brotherton, go ahead."

"God damn," Charlie said as he dismounted. He mumbled another curse as he got his mount to lie down.

At that spot, the prairie grass reached to mid-thigh on Addison. He knelt, and the mud soaked cold into his knees. Not enough to make him shiver. Outlaw shivered, though. "I know it's cold," he said in his put-a-baby-to-sleep voice. "You won't have to put up with it long. Nooooo."

Charlie was talking to his horse, too. That was good.

Was the rain slacking off? It was. The visibility would improve. That'd be good.

Then, "We shoulda' gone to Brotherton," Charlie bellyached.

16

Mariah said, "I don't want to go as a healer. I want to be a fighter."

Reedley stared at her and rubbed his chin. For a second. "All right. Get dressed. Properly. Then hustle back here and help us get ready to leave. We need to be out of here as soon as is humanly possible."

Ma Freeman grabbed Mariah's arm. "Come with me."

She led Mariah out of the bustle, onto Main Street, and next door to her own house.

"Take off your skirt." Ma left her daughter-in-law in the living room.

A moment later, Ma returned from her bedroom and held up a skirt that had been split in half, it appeared, and then sewn back together like bloomers.

"But Ma, this is like wearing pants."

"It is wearing pants. If you insist on going with Joshua Reedley, you're going to have to ride Percy astride, not side saddle. If wearing these," Ma held up the just finished garment, "offends you, stay here."

Mariah took the modified skirt and pulled it, or them, on. It was not a skirt or dress, rather pants or bloomers.

Uncomfortable, unseemly, unladylike. It did fit, though.

"During the journey here, before you and your family joined us, several of us women wore these. Including Mrs. Larrimer."

"The preacher's wife wore … bloomers? In public? In daylight?"

Ma nodded and smiled. Then the smile blinked off. "Joshua said you could stay here, that he'd send for you after the fighting."

"I need to go, Ma. I have to see something of what Addison does on these kinds of … outings."

"Mariah, you'll get over wearing this kind of garb in public. Some of the other things you see out there, you will never get over."

Mariah started to head for the door and stopped. "Hope is—"

"I know. Infant Care Center," Ma said. "Hurry."

Mariah ran past three wagons already parked in front of the Meeting House. At her house, she lit a lantern, hurried to the shed in back, and saddled Percy.

At the Meeting House, no wagons waited. Ma Freeman did.

"Reedley left with five wagons. He said he couldn't wait any longer. And he repeated, you can stay here. But if you decide to come, you have to push your horse hard to catch up."

Mariah slapped the reins across Percy's haunch. The animal seemed as surprised as she was at herself. They left Ma standing on the boardwalk.

She rode insanely fast in the dark, as she'd done back in Illinois. Three times. To help a woman deliver a midnight baby, she'd called them. She'd survived those gallops through the blackness by luck, her Pa said. Preacher said it was because God watched over her on her mission of service.

Mariah prayed and hoped for luck.

She remembered Addison talking about how, at night, it was better to look out of the sides of your eyes instead of straight ahead. She tried it.

Addison was right.

With her side vision, the black night turned into a gray one, and she could make out the edges of the road.

Percy slowed. Then she saw a wagon parked just to the left of the road. She reined Percy up next to it. In all, five wagons had been lined up tongue to tailgate.

Teams were being led away to her right. Men and women unloaded barricades and erected them on the southside of the wagons. One man stood in the bed of the wagon next to her, staring through binoculars to the south.

"Mariah." Joshua Reedley walked toward her. "Hop down."

Reedley took the reins and handed them to the oldest Fishboch boy. "Put her horse with the others."

Joshua then turned and pulled a rifle from the bed of the wagon next to them. "You know how to use this?"

Mariah nodded, then said, "Yes, sir."

"In daylight, right?"

"Well, yes."

"If you can't see a target, you'll see flashes of gunfire. Point the gun at those. Now, get behind the fifth barricade. You can use the end wagon as a medical aid post when the shootins done. And here, take a second rifle with you."

When she got to the end of the row, a man, and a woman, in a dress, were unhitching the team. All the draft and riding stock had been herded up about two-hundred yards clear of the wagons, back towards Brotherton. She'd passed them as she joined Reedley's gang and wondered why the horses were being kept there. Now it made sense. When they shot at the bushwhackers, the pro-slavers would shoot back. This would keep their animals clear of the enemy's fire. Hopefully.

"Mariah." It was a man from Preacher Cromwell's congregation. If she had a moment, she'd remember his name. "Get behind the barricade on the other side of the wagon. When the pro-slavers come, concentrate on the ones to our far right. Shoot kneeling down with your rifle through a hole. Never stick your head above the barricade. When the shooting starts, you might get excited, but do not forget 'Do not stand up.' Understand?"

She took her place between a man and another woman, both Cromwell people. After kneeling, sticking her rifle through the hole, squinting down the barrel, and seeing nothing, not even the end of her weapon, she leaned back on her heels.

All the frantic activity to get there, to be part of this fight, then go from that to just waiting. She thought she was ready to be a fighter but hadn't been prepared for waiting.

Now, no more than a minute into it, she began to doubt her preparedness for—.

Ambush was the word her mind almost formed, but that word seemed, all of a sudden, too polite. Killing. That was the word that needed contemplation.

Mariah the healer was now Mariah the killer.

The Healer hid behind a barricade wearing a belt gun and holding a rifle, prepared to kill or wound. And she wore pants! Ma Freeman was right. Mariah would never forget this night. And the shooting hadn't started yet.

She glanced to her right and left.

Do they wonder if they'll be able to kill someone, too?

Her husband had killed, yet at home, Addison was a considerate, loving husband and father.

How was it possible to be a killer in one place, and a kind man at home?

She reminded herself of the earlier bushwhacker raids. On one of them, the pro-slavers intended to kill the men, women, and children of Brotherton. Then, they would scalp their victims and receive a bounty for each hank of hair collected. Even Hope would not have been safe from the vicious predators!

In many ways, what she was doing was protecting Hope and all the people in Brotherton from cruel deaths. Still, she felt as if she had already killed and now was trying to justify what she'd done. Justify an unjustifiable act.

Reedley's voice boomed, "Keep your mind on the business we are about here. Stay behind the barricades. Shoot through the rifle holes. Don't shoot until I holler 'Fire!' When I do holler, keep shooting till you're empty. Then pick up another gun and shoot till it's empty. If I holler 'Cease Fire,' stop shooting. Immediately."

It seemed simple enough. The waiting wasn't easy, though. The bothersome thoughts continued to nag, even knowing an invisible enemy advanced toward her, hidden by the blackest night she'd ever witnessed. At least the rain had stopped.

Reedley chopped off the waiting. "Get ready."

Noise. A herd of horses. Coming right at her. Peering through the rifle hole, Mariah couldn't see them.

They sound so close! Dear Lord ....

She checked her gun. It was cocked. Her finger slipped over the trigger.

At the same instant, shapes of mounted men solidified close and huge in front of her, and "Fire!" at wake-the-dead level boomed.

She closed her eyes and pulled the trigger. Shook her head, to clear it, jacked in another round. This time, she squeezed the trigger while aiming at a man.

Bullets thwacked into the logs in front of her. Horses screamed and whinnied. Men cursed.

Through her peephole, horses reared and fell. Riders flew backward off their saddles. Bushwhacker gunfire flashed in the blackness. The screaming, cursing, booming cacophony rumbled like it would go on forever. Mariah vaguely noticed the sights and sounds. She fired her rifle, again, and again, and again. When her hammer fell twice without causing the weapon to kick her shoulder, she picked up the rifle next to her and stuck it through the hole. Pull the trigger. Work the lever. Squeeze the trigger. Her hammer clicked on empty again, when "Cease fire! Cease fire!" cut through the invisible fog in Mariah's head.

Mariah started to stand up but then remembered, *Don't stand up.* The man and the woman next to her stood. The woman crumpled into a heap as gunfire flashed and thundered anew.

Reedley hollered, "Fire! Fire! Resume firing! Resume firing!"

The banging and popping burst out. Mariah squatted back on her haunches, drawing her face farther back from the barricade, stuck her pistol through the hole, and squeezed. Thumb cock. Aim a bit to the left. Squeeze. Cock and fire again. Aim a tweak right. Fire, cock, fire. She emptied the gun, reloaded, and shot six more times. She was reloading when, "Cease fire. Cease firing," came.

Mariah huffed breaths out and in through her open mouth. She licked her lips. Thirsty. She felt like she was asleep and watching a dream of herself, but this dream she watched from outside herself, not from inside like all the other times.

The woman!

She lay on her side. Mariah rolled her onto her back and felt for a pulse. No pulse. She placed her hand on her chest. Not breathing.

"Healer to the middle barricade!" Reedley. "Crawl, Mariah. Do not stand up."

As if I needed that warning!

But she did need it. Tears flooded up from the belly of her soul and threatened to burst loose. Stopping that gush hurt her throat, and for a moment, she thought she might vomit, but that impulse, too, she muscled into submission. And crawled. And thanked Ma Freeman for her woman pants.

A dog howled. Close. The O'Riley's wolfhound?

"Mariah. You comin'?" Reedley.

She opened her mouth, but no sound came out. After forcing her dry mouth to swallow, "Coming."

The dog howled again. Mariah shivered and kept crawling. She found a man lying on his back. Joshua Reedley knelt by his head. Another man, one of the O'Riley twins, squatted between the victim and the barricade. He had his arm around the wolfhound.

"Sean was holding the leash." The dog holder wailed more than said. "When the bushwhackers got close, Dog tried to get at them and jerked on the leash. Stupid couldn't hold his aim through the porthole and rested his rifle atop the barricade. I told him to get down, but would he listen? Stupid would not."

In the starlight, she could see a trail of dark fluid had leaked from the twin's, Sean's, right eye. Mariah checked for a pulse and sign of breathing and found neither.

"Sorry, Mr. O'Riley," Mariah said.

"Thank ye, Lass. I know."

From behind the next barricade toward Brotherton, Marvin Dinwiddie called to Reedley: "Got two wounded here. An arm and a leg."

Reedley sent Mariah back to the end wagon. Ma Freeman had loaded medical supplies for her while she'd been saddling Percy.

*****

Addison checked on Charlie. He was behind his horse. It lay quiet. The rain had stopped. That was good. Visibility was some better Facing east again, he caught movement in the corner of his eye. He made out two riders coming right at him and Charlie. Outriders.

"Charlie, two riders coming. You got 'em?"

"Uhn—"

"Peripheral vision! Remember?"

"Got 'em."

"I'll take the one on the left," Addison said. "You get the other one. I'll wait until you fire."

"Uhn—"

"If you think your man is close, wait. If you think he's too close, shoot."

Charlie rose to his knees and put his rifle to his shoulder.

Wait. Wait.

Addison pictured his gunsights. He pictured lining them up on his target. He put his finger on the trigger. *The target was close. Closer. Too—*. Charlie fired, and Addison flinched. He had to re-picture his gunsights. Then he fired with his target practically on top of him. His man went over backwards off the saddle. The other man was firing a pistol. Charlie fired again. He missed again. Addison knocked Charlie's target out of the saddle.

Charlie stood. "God damn," and pointed. "The whole damned army is coming at us."

Addison looked. Charlie was sort of right. Probably ten men. "Outlaw," he said, and his horse got to its feet. Before mounting, he fired two rounds at the gaggle. In the middle of the bunched riders, a horse went down. The rest kept coming. Time to get out of here. Charlie was already hightailing it away.

Addison slipped the rifle sling over his chest and swung up onto the saddle. Outlaw tore out after Charlie.

Outlaw was catching up to Charlie.

The thunder of gunfire rumbled behind him. He turned and glanced behind, but he couldn't see anything. The firing had stopped. Had the pursuers given up?

Then, the sound of gunfire kicked up again. A lot of it. It sounded like two thunderstorms arguing with each other.

Had Brotherton sent a party out to ambush the pro-slavers before they attacked the town?

Addison reined up and turned. Those who had been chasing him now rode toward the sound of shooting. He and Outlaw watched until, after a time, the booming and banging flittered out.

*****

Reedley sent Hermann Vogelsang to rig up some extra bullet shields for the last wagon. There was no way to totally block the light of a lantern. Additional riflemen were also deployed to defend that end of the line.

As Mariah arrived at the end wagon, Bushwhackers wailed for help out of the darkness.

"Help. There's some of us shot bad."

Reedley's voice answered. "You want help, walk or crawl here to the barricades."

The voice said none of them could move.

"Then we'll come look for you after the sun comes up. Don't trust you in daylight, and sure don't in the dark."

Two of the Brotherton fighters had suffered flesh wounds. She bandaged their injuries and made them as comfortable she could on the ground.

The pitiful pleading continued from the darkness. "In the outer darkness, where there will be weeping and gnashing of teeth," came to mind. That was no longer one of the phrases from the Bible that did not have meaning at a visceral level.

Just before midnight, the first wounded bushwhacker was dragged to Mariah's medical aid station. She wound up bandaging seven of them, but the pleading from other wounded continued from the darkness.

Mariah got to sleep about two thirty and woke again at three thirty. It was deathly quiet. No more pleading. She was pretty sure what that meant.

Hope and Addison, Lord, please watch over them.

Her eyes closed again and stayed that way until the sun opened them.

17

After the gunfire abruptly quit, Addison and Outlaw continued to stare toward the east. Above, a few stars found holes in the overcast to peek through. A gentle breeze wafted over him from the west. Except when a storm threatened, western winds normally blew.

Normal.

There was a time when the word held safety, security, the comfort of being at home every night. Since Found Grace Church left Illinois, fighting, shooting, killing had become what was normal. What he'd been called to do, though, protected Mariah and Hope, and Brotherton.

"Maybe I should wish for … pray for the abnormal. Or the old normal."

The horse bobbed his head up and down. Outlaw was a good listener, and sometimes he even had answers.

"Charlie. Last we saw of him; he was hightailing it west. He's probably halfway to Oregon by now."

A snort answered that last thought. Abruptly, Outlaw tensed; his ears twitched forward.

He tugged the reins and softly said, "Down."

Addison heard it then. More than one rider, probably at a gallop.

When he hunkered down himself, he squatted behind the saddle with Outlaw's legs pointed toward what or whom they were hiding from. A horse lying down and rising to its feet was not a thing of grace and beauty. If he had to get him to his feet in a hurry, it was prudent to be clear of the animal's legs.

Addison listened and stared at the approaching sound. It seemed like every time, he had to remind himself that peripheral vision was superior to straight-ahead eyesight at night. He turned his head a tweak. He still couldn't see the approaching riders. Probably two. Outlaw raised his head off the ground. Addison drew a pistol.

He saw them then. Two riders. Abreast. Coming right at them. "Stay down."

Addison stood, pulling his other pistol. "Rein up," he hollered.

One of the horses reared, and its rider tumbled backward over the animal's rump.

The other horse skidded to a stop, and its rider fired. A bullet zipped past Addison. He fired both pistols, and the man dropped off the side of his mount.

Addison ran to the man he hadn't shot. He lay on his back, panting, his hands up at about ear level.

"You's that damned white Injun Wes told us about."

"Was I you, mister," Addison said, "I'd listen real careful. Do not move a muscle unless I tell you to. Then, make it slow and easy. Understand?"

No answer.

This time louder. "Understand?" And with hard edges.

"Yeah. No sudden moves. Slow and easy."

"Just that way, pull off your left boot and drop it."

He grunted getting each of them off. Addison kicked them away, and said, "stand up."

The man got to his feet, about as gracefully as a laying-down horse.

"So," Addison said, "Wes made it back to you. How's he doing?"

"Wes got a busted arm and leg."

Addison pulled the man's belt guns and tossed them by the boots.

"We left him with some grub and told him we'd pick him up after we burned Brotherton to the ground."

Addison pulled the man's shoulder holster weapons.

"Hah!" the man said. "This is the third time me and Orv tried to burn down Brotherton. 'They're just eastern pilgrims. They'll be easy.' That's what we all thought, but ever time we get whupped bad. Well, me and Orv had enough. We're heading for California."

The bushwhacker paused for a moment, then continued, "Uh, Orv. I heard shooting."

"We'll check on him."

"Put your hands up and start walking toward that ground-hitched bronc."

Orv lay face down.

"Kin I …" the prisoner said.

"Slow and easy,"

Orv's partner knelt and turned him over. There was enough light to make out the black stain on his chest.

"Goddamn," the kneeler said.

"Stand up," Addison said. He stood. "What's your name?"

"Uh. Uh."

"You don't know your own name?"

"Jack. It's Jack."

"Last name?"

"Uh … Schmitt. I'm Jack Schmitt."

Addison stood and stared at the man, a dark shadow against an even darker background.

"Uh, anything wrong?" Jack Schmitt said.

Again, Addison waited to respond until even he got uncomfortable with the duration of it. Then, "Yeah, Uh-Jack-Schmitt, there is."

Waiting out yet another pause, Uh-Jack-Schmitt shifted his weight from one foot to the other and back.

"This was your third raid against the people of Brotherton, you said. You were given a parole on the first or the second, weren't you?" Before the man could answer, "You were given a parole on the first raid. On the second, you gave a different name. That right?"

"No!" More a shouted plea than a loud answer. "I … uh. I never got no parole."

"Tell me your real name, and what you tell me better be something that smells like the truth, or I'll shoot you where you stand."

"Wait. Wait!"

Addison cocked the hammer.

"My name is Abel Conway."

"And Abel Conway busted parole. What name did you use for the second one?"

"Uh, well—"

"What name?"

"Clem Davis."

Addison shot him. His pistol arm dropped, limp, to his side. It was the first time he'd executed a man. All the other men he'd killed had fired at him, or threatened to shoot.

Joshua Reedley, Ziggy Hostetler, and his own blood brother had all shot unarmed parole breakers. Jibway had even killed one when it had clearly been Addison's job to do so, it was just that Addison wrestled with balancing how wrong it was to shoot an unarmed man with how wrong it was to break the sacred word of a parole. And he hadn't had it worked out yet when his blood brother saved him from further dithering.

But Jibway wasn't there this time to save him from the moral burden. The spiritual weight of what he'd done caused his shoulders to droop. His soul, he thought, was like a room filled with light from a dozen lamps, and someone had turned out half of them.

Addison!

Jibway's stern voice called him to pay attention to his surroundings, with pro-slavers prowling in the darkness.

He took a deep breath, huffed it out, and stood up straight. Slowly, he looked all around with his ears and with his eyes, concentrating on using peripheral vision. He sensed nothing threatening.

"Outlaw."

The horse came to him, and Addison felt another notch better, with Outlaw's eyes, ears, and nose at work.

"That shooting we heard," he said softly. "It had to be Joshua

Reedley bushwhacking the bushwhackers. It's the only thing that makes sense."

The horse just stood there. Looking east.

"Do you agree with me?" he whispered. "If you disagree, just don't neigh."

Addison snorted trying to contain the laughter that bubbled up from the belly of his soul.

If you agree, don't neigh. Funny as all get out.

Then it hit him like a horse kick in the belly.

"Father God, Lord of heaven and earth." In a whisper. "I just executed a man, and then I laughed. Forgive this trespass and save me from having to ever do it again."

Outlaw head bumped Addison on the arm.

Amen.

Sunup was still a long way off. It wouldn't do to fumble around in the dark looking for Joshua Reedley's gang. He'd likely get shot. *Serve me—*

This time, he did not need the voice of his blood brother to put his mind to work on his situation. He spread his ground cloth, looped a rope around Outlaw's neck, tied the rope to his wrist, lay down, and exhaustion pulled him below the surface of the lake of sleep.

*****

A tug on his wrist jerked Addison to wakefulness. He snatched a pistol from a holster near his head and rolled to his knees. Outlaw stared … east. The sun hung above the hazy horizon.

Good hour past sunrise.

Outlaw did not seem concerned. He just thought it was high time I woke the heck up.

Addison stood, slipped into his shoulder holster, buckled on his belt gun, and donned his hat. Then he scanned the horizon, the full circle. "Nothing to worry about, eh, Outlaw?" The horse bent his head and bit off a mouthful of grass.

Mariah. And Hope. Sunrise always roused the baby. He rolled

up the ground cloth and thought of sleeping in a bed, with a little luck, that night.

Abel Conway appeared inside his head. Thou shalt not kill.

Maybe Lord, there should be a "comma but" after that one.

The penance pew in New Found Grace Church came to mind. Preachers Larrimer and Cromwell would plonk him on that bench for a good spell if he started appending "comma buts" onto the commandments God gave Moses.

"Whadda you say, Outlaw? You ready to go and checkout what all that shooting was about last night?"

The horse eased his forelegs forward and stretched his hindlegs rearward. Addison stepped back.

When the horse was finished, Addison led him clear of the puddle and got some jerky from a saddle bag. After the sun was high enough so he wouldn't be "white man stupid," as his blood brother termed riding into a rising sun, Addison set off toward Brotherton with Outlaw at a lope. A lope ate distance but afforded the opportunity for careful observation. Scattered bushwhackers could be about. Joshua Reedley might have—would have scouts out, and they might be "white man stupid," and shoot first and say, "Who's there?" second.

That morning, mist and fog rising from the rain-soaked earth limited visibility, but he figured he could still see for two or three miles.

He'd been riding a little less than an hour when the hair on the back of his neck tingled. After he reined to a stop, Outlaw craned his neck around and one-eye looked at his rider. The look in the horse's eye said, "Why'd we stop?"

"Morning, Pilgrim," came from behind him.

Addison dove off the saddle, hit the ground, rolled onto his belly, and rose with a pistol in each hand. To find Jibway laughing his fool head off.

"White man stupid mean same as white man funny," the Indian said.

Jibway didn't wear a hat, but that morning, he wore a crown of prairie grass secured to his head by a leather thong. His clothing was the color of the drought-browned grass.

"You didn't smell him?" Addison asked Outlaw.

Jibway laughed and threw a horse biscuit at Addison. "More white man funny. He blame horse."

His blood brother had rubbed horse manure on his clothes and under his arms to hide his man scent.

Addison shook his head. Also, getting the last word with the Injun was a most unlikely proposition. He looked in the direction they'd been riding, then turned back. "You ambushed the bushwhackers last night?"

"We did. Joshua Reedley had us load some of Otto Vogelsang's barricades in wagons, and we set up just this side of the Trail. Surprised the hell out of them." Jibway busted out laughing again. "About like you got surprised."

Addison stood with his arms at his side, a pistol in each hand. He holstered and waited to see if he'd have to absorb more ridicule.

"Reedley and the wagons are about three miles ahead of you," Jibway said. "Ride on, and you'll see them soon."

"You want to ride double?"

"No. I'll stay here. Maybe you get breakfast and come back and take over here. Oh, and Mariah's there."

"Mariah was part of the ambush?"

He didn't wait for an answer but swung up onto Outlaw and set off at a gallop.

After about a mile, a line of wagons took shape out of the fog and haze. He slowed to a lope. A moment later, Outlaw stopped and cocked his ears forward.

"I'm Addison Freeman," he shouted.

Orson Seiling rose out of the grass. "Hold it down, Addison Freeman. Folks is sleeping in those wagons. They been up all night."

"Figured Reedley would have somebody out here watching. Didn't want you to mistake me for a bushwhacker and shoot me." Addison sniffed. "Bacon! If you do decide to shoot me, could you wait till after breakfast?"

"Sure," Orson said, "we caught three wounded parole violaters. After we serve them breakfast, we're gonna serve them a firing squad. We'll gist put you in line with them."

His mind formed Long as I get breakfast first, but he didn't say it. It wasn't a thing to joke about. At his Tsk, tsk, Outlaw set off, again at a lope.

Five wagons were lined up tongue to tail. In front of the wagons, a half dozen plank barricades had been erected. Room for three riflemen behind each! Reedley set up a good ambush.

Marshal McTavish stood next to the end wagon closest to Brotherton. By way of greeting, he said, "Where's Charlie?"

Deputy Town Marshal Freeman, paused, trying to frame the right kind of response. "We were running from a handful of bushwhackers. Riding west. Charlie was out in front of me. Outlaw stumbled. I feared he was lamed up. I managed to ambush the bushwhackers. Last I saw, Charlie was—he almost said hightailing, but it sounded too much like the marshal's son was running from a fight—heading west."

"He's alright, then?"

"For as I know. Uh. Marshal, is Mariah here?"

"Yep. She's by the wagon at the other end of the row. Got her a little hospital set up there."

None of the wagons wore a canvas cover over the bed except the one on the far end. Addison rode there and hopped down. Mariah was bandaging splints to a man's thigh. The man's pants leg had been cut away.

"Mariah!" Addison said.

She looked at him and smiled big and warm.

"What are you doing here?" Addison's words came out laced with accusation.

As soon as he said the words and heard his tone of voice, he regretted saying them. They'd struck her like a slap. Her smile clouded over.

"I'm busy," she said.

There was way more dismissal in her words than there'd been remonstrance in his.

"Hope," he said, "who's—"

"Your mother. Now leave! This is not the time or the place."

Now he felt like she'd slapped him. *Don't you see how much it scared me to think you were out here? On an ambush!*

He slunk away like a tail-tucked dog. Inside his head, though, the kettle of simmering anger boiled over. *What were you thinking Mariah? You should be back in Brotherton with our baby.* When they did get to the proper place and time to talk about this, he fully intended to put her firmly in her place. The thought of switching her as Pa had beat him so many times flitted through his mind. He shook his head to keep that thought moving right on through.

Someone snickered.

Hermann Vogelsang stood beside the next wagon in line wearing a big grin. "Easy to see who wear da pants in your family."

Addison stopped, his right fist clenched, and faced the bigger man. Someone grabbed his left arm, and he started to swing a punch in that direction. But it was Preacher Cromwell. His punch stopped half-thrown.

Cromwell let go of Addison's arm, said, "Follow me," turned, and started walking away.

Addison's fist opened. The hand dropped to his side. His head was filled with nothing but jumbled emotion, with not a single coherent thought, except for "Follow me." His feet responded to that.

ddison followed Preacher Cromwell with no clear thought in his head except to do just that. But the preacher kept walking. Out of the muddle roiling between his forehead and the back of his skull: *Should be beyond earshot by now.* Earshot. A term Cromwell's people used.

Addison looked behind him. The wagons were far enough away a shout would be heard, but not a normal conversation.

"Preacher Cromwell, where are we going?"

The man of God stopped. He turned. Removing his flat-brimmed hat, he rubbed his forehead as if the frown wrinkles hurt.

"I was looking for a log to sit on." He shook his head. "I forgot we are in Kansas. Here, if you want a log to sit on, you have to bring it with you."

Bitterness gilded the words of the last sentence. He had expected the preacher to guide him from befuddlement back to—that word again—normalcy. But just then, Cromwell seemed in need of guidance every bit as much as Addison did.

"The conversation I wanted, or maybe needed, to have with you, I had it in my head that it should be conducted sitting down." Cromwell put his hat back on and faced east. Remember when you talked to me that day in our camp on the far bank of the Missouri River?"

Addison remembered. He nodded.

"My mind was so twisted up with indignation at the west, and western people, I couldn't think straight. I saw you all this way.

"It is winter, and you are riding down a road. You come across a man huddled by a fire. The man is wearing a thin outer coat, inadequate for the cold. You are wearing a heavy coat and have another heavy one tied behind your saddle. Do you, Western Man, give the man your spare coat? You do not. You shoot him and take his thin coat and wear it under your heavy one."

Addison wasn't sure where the conversation was going, but he thought the preacher had been right. The conversation would have been more comfortable sitting rather than standing. Then: *You shoot him and take his thin coat* penetrated the fog in his head. He'd shot unarmed Abel Conway. Was this eastern preacher saying shooting a two-time parole braker was the same as shooting a helpless man for his thin coat when he already had two thick ones?

Indignation sparked as clear as a shaft of lightning out of an approaching dark night storm.

Preacher Cromwell sucked in a big breath and huffed it out. "When you spoke with me back there in Missouri, you enabled me to see that there were some cold-blooded savages in the west, but, also, the west was occupied by God-fearing, good-hearted, salt-of-the-earth people as well. The land out here is hard and primitive and can turn you hard and cruel. But you don't have to allow that to happen. You can do what you must to survive while. at the same time, retaining your Christianity. You taught me that."

Addison's indignation fizzled. He had followed the preacher seeking the restoration of order to his jumble of confused thoughts. But was the preacher saying he was the one confused?

Cromwell looked east again. "Back there," he pointed, "I called our church to join me on a Journey of Salvation. To here in Kansa. Where we'd vote to end the abomination of slavery. Every man and woman in the congregation believed it was an abomination for men to own other men as if they were cattle. Half my people refused to join me. One of the refusers was Clotilde, my wife."

Wait! The preacher's wife …

"You are a good man, Addison Freeman."

Addison's mind had locked onto the preacher's wife's refusal. Crowell had said something, but it registered as a mumble.

Preacher Cromwell gripped Addison's shoulders and looked him hard in one eye, then in the other. "You take up the hard, unpleasant jobs filled with the heaviest of moral consequence. Afterward, you show your soul to God and ask Him to help you deal with what you've done."

"But your wife, Clotilde?"

A sigh. "Yes. She said this land was an abomination peopled by uncivilized, godless, soulless white men and soulless red heathens who worship their version of the golden calf. Best to let these two factions kill each other off."

Neither nor Cromwell smiled much. He'd considered thinking *ever* but rejected that.

Cromwell smiled. "Your mouth is hanging open, Mr. Freeman."

Mr. Freeman closed it.

"Truth be told, Clotilde grew up in a life of privilege and comfort. She did have a spark of independence and of the rebel, though, and that's how we wound up married, despite the strenuous objection of her father."

Addison had followed Preacher Cromwell expecting to bare his soul, but the preacher had just bared his! It was hard for his mind to wrap itself around all he'd said.

"Mariah is a pearl beyond price, Addison. You see that, don't you? And you surely see that God meant for you two to be together. Otherwise, why would He have orchestrated your coming together in the most extraordinary way?"

Did he know Mariah had gotten with child by Orson?

Cromwell smiled again.

He knew. He placed his hands on Addison's shoulders again. "Go to her."

There were times when a preacher ended a pronouncement with "my son," and it annoyed Addison. Now, he hadn't said those two words, and, this time, he wished the preacher had.

*****

Mariah paused bandaging the man's head. For a moment, she watched her husband walk toward the bunch of prisoners she'd already treated. His reaction to finding her there had surprised her. The apology equally surprised. He knelt, said the words, rose, and went on about his business! The healer returned attention to her current patient. Part of it, anyway.

Addison was a good man. He'd loved her even during … the infatuation with Orson. Pa Freeman wanted to arrange a marriage between them, but Addison refused because he knew she did not love him as he loved her. *But then, after I found out I was with child, and that Orson was already married, Addison wedded me. And saved me. And saved Hope.*

But, his reaction to seeing her with the ambush party? Then it dawned. He wanted me safe, back in Brotherton with the baby. Doesn't he know how much I worry about him when he's gone?

The most important thing was his apology had opened a way for them to talk. Hopefully tonight. Please, God, tonight?

*****

In all, Addison's crew piled nineteen dead pro-slavers into two wagons. Butchered horse meat filled another two.

Back at the pro-slaver cemetery to the west of Pott's Trading Post, other prisoners and Brotherton citizens dug graves. Otto Vogelsang and his son Hermann carved names into pieces of wood for marking the graves. Many of the existing markers read, "He said his name was … ." But for this gang of bushwhackers, one of the dead, Mort Mundt, had been identified as the leader of the group. In one of his pockets, they found a list with fifty-four names on it. Twenty-one of the names also appeared on Joshua Reedley's list of parolees. Six of the parole violators were among the wounded captives. Which meant twenty-five graves were needed.

Addison arrived at the cemetery with the wagons, bushwhacker prisoners, and mounted and armed men and women from Brotherton guarding the pro-slavers.

Marshal McTavish waited on the west side of the gathering. Addison reined up in front of him.

"Which one of your prisoners is the parole breaker?" the marshal asked.

Addison pointed to a horse-meat-wagon driver. McTavish ordered the man to join five other bushwhackers sitting on the ground guarded by townsmen. A separate gaggle, about a dozen and also under guard, sat huddled in another circle.

An unhitched wagon had been parked before the newly dug graves. Preachers Cromwell and Larrimer stood on the bed and faced the crowd, comprised of most of the town. A restrained mumble issued from them.

Preacher Cromwell raised his arms. Men removed their hats. Mothers shushed their children. Fathers nudged their sons to remove their caps.

"Oh, Lord our God, we lift up our thanksgiving," Cromwell's outside-church preaching voice had no trouble making itself heard. "We thank You for delivering us from yet another attack from the pro-slavery people."

Preacher Larrimer's deeper voice rumbled, "As with the previous assaults, they intended to wipe us out. To kill every Brotherton man, woman, and child, and then to burn our town to the ground. During our Holy Crusade, we had to become holy warriors because we did not travel here to Kansas. We fought our way here."

Cromwell said, "Our journey to the Kansas territory was different. We boated down the Ohio and up the Missouri and were shielded from the anti-abolitionists and pro-slavers." He paused. "Until we stepped ashore in Atchison. Then, the hate and deadly nature of our antagonists hit us like a stampede of wild horses. But, a sort of Joshua, like Moses' Joshua, showed me the kind of the people and land we'd come to. He showed me the real hard nature of Kansas and some of its people. He showed me how to fight the hate and deadly cruelty, and as long as I held onto my God and savior, I would not allow the fighting to turn myself cruel and heartless."

Me, a sort of Joshua?

"Of course," Larrimer took over, "we have a real Joshua, and thank You, Lord, for planting Joshua Reedley in Found Grace Church. Without him, we would not have made it halfway across Illinois. Without him, there would be no Brotherton. Without him, Brotherton would not have survived. For our brother and Biblical Joshua, thank You, Lord."

The congregation responded, "For this blessing. Thank You, Lord."

Addison wondered if Reedley was there. Joshua would not have wanted Preacher Larrimer publicly praising him to high heaven.

Cromwell: "We came through another battle with the pro-slavers."

Larrimer: "But this time, we paid a terrible price. We lost Sean O'Riley."

Cromwell: "And we lost Eileen Nelson. A wife. Mother of two. And our sister."

Larrimer: "We will conduct their funerals tomorrow morning at eight. Now, Marshal McTavish has something to say."

The marshal put on his hat, climbed up a front wagon wheel, stepped into the driver's box, and faced the crowd. "Over there." He pointed. "Those six men attacked us before. We captured them, and if each one promised never to attack us again, we paroled that man. They all promised, but these returned with murder still in their hearts.

"There is only one punishment for parole breakers."

Addison had been about to dismount, but the heavy hush that settled over the battlefield stayed him. He held his breath.

What in blue blazes are you doing, McTavish? Was the marshal about to involve the men and women from town in killing the parole breakers?

Not the way to do this.

The women and younger ones should be sent back to town, and men who'd been in fights before should be selected to do the job.

Timothy O'Riley's, "I'll kill 'em," shattered the brittle silence. "I'll shoot them all."

Addison huffed out his held breath.

O'Riley stood in the center of the first row of the crowd. He glared up at McTavish. "With Sean's pistol," which he brandished.

Mayor Gallant Argyl grabbed O'Riley's arm.

Timothy swung a looping roundhouse punch, which the mayor easily blocked. O'Riley froze except for the silent sobs bobbing his shoulders heartbeat-fast. The wolfhound howled like the devil bit his tail.

A shiver ascended Addison's spine and prickled the hairs on the back of his neck.

"Come with me." The mayor led Timothy away, the dog at O'Riley's heel.

The eyes of the assembly followed the threesome until they had gone a dozen or so paces beyond the edge of the crowd. Then Marshal McTavish reclaimed their attention.

"We have business to conduct," the marshal thundered. "I ask for a dozen volunteers for a firing squad."

"I volunteer."

McTavish spun around. "Preacher Cromwell, you don't have to—"

The man of God elevated his chin. "I volunteer."

From the crowd, "I volunteer," snapped Addison's head left. Mariah!

From atop Outlaw, Addison saw men frown, women raise hands to their mouths, and frowning husbands and open-mouthed wives look at each other.

Maybell Jim volunteered, followed quickly by about two dozen males.

Marshal McTavish said, "Preacher Cromwell, Mariah, Maybell, and I'll pick the nine best shots from the rest of you."

No, Mariah! Some spirit power kept that thought from shooting out of Addison's mouth like a cannonball.

When he'd executed Abel Conway, he felt empty. Just empty. Once he decided he had to shoot the three-time parole breaker, he became a hollowed-out statue. His stomach was empty from the top of his head to the soles of his feet. All thought, save one, Shoot the oath violator, fled his mind. And the emptiness, it was cold.

Dearest Mariah. You are a healer, a saver of lives. You are kind and caring. You are not a cold-blooded killer.

Like me.

But Addison could not intervene again. Not after chastising her, and then, with Preacher Cromwell's help, apologizing. Neither could he stay and watch her look down the barrel of her rifle at a man.

He reined Outlaw around to skirt the crowd and headed back to Brotherton. As much as an infant needed her mother, so much did he need Hope.

Addison knocked on the door to his mother's house.

"Come in."

Ma sat in the rocker. Hope was in her arms. The baby's face wore a serious expression as she stared up at her grandmother, almost as if Hope knew today it was her job to comfort this older woman.

"Mariah?" Ma said.

"She's okay." Addison frowned.

"What is it?"

Addison stared at the hat in his hand for a moment. "We're executing some parole breakers. She volunteered to be in the firing squad."

"What! Holy Mother of God, pray for Mariah."

A sound, like a single clap of thunder, muted by distance, rolled across the prairie from the west.

"Ma, let me hold her, please."

He took his daughter and had to restrain himself from crushing her to him. With Hope in his arms and looking up at him, love, caring, concern, warm good things flooded his heart, and moved out the cold emptiness abiding there.

Addison circled the living room twice and stopped in front of his mother, still in the rocker.

"I have to get back." He handed over his daughter.

"You just got here, son. Stay. Just a bit longer."

"I can't, Ma."

She nodded. "You have to get back to Mariah."

There were twenty-five graves to fill and paroles to offer to the dozen or so prisoners. He had no idea what to do about, with, or for Mariah. He could handle the graves and the paroles. If any of those refused to give their parole, they would have to be shot, too. One thing was clear: Addison did not want Mariah to have to kill any more men.

*****

Joshua Reedley's list of paroles wound up shortened considerably. Half the men listed on Mort Mundt's roster were parolees, and all but a handful of them had been killed. Addison shoveled dirt into the grave of one of the parole breakers. Then Marshal McTavish wanted him to help interview the eleven prisoners whose fates still needed to be determined.

The marshal, Joshua Reedley, and Addison interrogated the pro-slavers one by one. When the interviews were completed, all the raiding party survivors promised to never again bear arms against the people of Brotherton. They were granted paroles, and Reedley entered their names into his ledger. The new parolees were then released. Each had a horse, a pistol, and provisions. As the sorry-looking lot rode away to the southeast, Addison thought he ought to say a prayer for them, but his mind refused to manufacture appropriate words.

That evening, communal supper was served in the Meeting House. Addison entered the hall and searched for his wife. She was not there. But Ma was.

"Sally Wilson is having her baby," Ma said. "Mariah is helping her."

Ma rose from her chair. "Sit here, son. I'll get you a plate."

The other people at the full table rose. Addison frowned.

Viola Dinwiddie said, "Sorry to leave you to eat alone, but church service starts in twenty minutes."

Ma returned with mashed potatoes, string beans, and horse meat. He didn't think he was hungry, but the vittles vacated the plate as rapidly as Viola had left the table.

When Addison entered the church, he found every pew crammed. Children sat on the laps of parents and older siblings. Young men occupied the aisles against both side walls. Before this latest pro-slavery raid demanded attention, the Town Council had approved expanding Brotherton to a seventh street and constructing another church. Otto Vogelsang was anxious to start the project, but it would have to wait. Funerals would take up tomorrow.

Addison joined the queue of standers. He leaned against the west wall, and all his remaining strength and energy drained into his boots.

"Good people of Brotherton," ended Addison's nap.

Nobody sleeps during a Preacher Larrimer sermon!

"Today, once again, the pro-slavery … advocates attacked us. With the express purpose of exterminating us. But," If anyone had managed to fall asleep, that *But* would have rousted them out of slumber, "Once again, Our Savior God guided our holy warriors to smite our enemies. This time, though, at a great cost. We lost our brother Sean and our sister Eileen. We will lay them to rest tomorrow. Now, we have another loss to absorb. Caleb Cromwell wishes to address us from the Penance Pew."

Caleb Cromwell? Not Preacher Cromwell?

No one uttered a word. A few nervous throats were cleared. A few restless feet scraped boots across floorboards.

Preacher Larrimer gestured toward the backless bench positioned between the preacher's and deacon's podiums.

Caleb seemed like a curse word in front of the man's last name. Mister wasn't any better. The man was Preacher Cromwell, pure and simple, and forever. Addison looked down at his hands as if what was happening here were their fault.

"I confess to you, Preacher Larrimer, and to you, my brothers and sisters, that I have sinned grievously. Against God, and against you." As the penitent swept the congregation with his gaze, his eyes spilled some of the pain he so obviously felt. "I had to go on the ambush. I could no longer stay here in Brotherton while the rest of you did the hard work of defending us. Putting not only your lives on the line but your souls as well. To defend us, you have to kill men. Men created and loved by God. Never mind they were led astray by the devil, who filled their hearts with lust for killing. When their bodies lie in the grave and look up at you, they are exactly that. Men created and loved by God. And yes, their faces were covered when we shoveled dirt onto them, but I could still see their faces."

Mister Cromwell hung his head for a moment. When he raised his eyes, they glistened. "Brothers and sisters, I know now, I feel now, the weight of the lives I've taken. For the first time, I understand the burdens you bear, those of you who have been forced to kill. I am so weighed down by this unbearable weight, I am unable to help anyone else bear their load. That is why I cannot serve as your preacher any longer.

"Last night, during the ambush, when we fired at the pro-slavers from behind the barricades, such a coldness filled my soul. I fired my gun at men and felt no hesitation, felt no remorse, felt less than I would have in shooting a squirrel for my supper. And then, during the firing squad, it really struck me, the total absence of remorse. I had become a cold-blooded killer.

"Please forgive me."

"I forgive you." Mariah stood at the rear of church; tears streamed down her cheeks. "Will you forgive me, please?"

Addison went to her but stopped himself from touching her, afraid she'd reject him; but she stepped to him, leaned against him, and his arms knew what to do.

*****

After services concluded, Ma Freeman offered to keep Hope overnight, but both parents wanted their child with them. Ma returned to her home. Mariah and Addison walked down B Street to Main. Mariah carried Hope. Addison led Outlaw and Percy.

All the houses along Main Street were dark; then, one by one, matches were put to wicks, and windows spilled light.

Addison stopped walking. *Put out those lamps!* formed as a thought that wanted to be shouted. Outlaw nudged him in the back. Addison started walking again. *We're home! We're safe!* These thoughts formed tinged with notes of incredulity.

They passed the five houses to get to their home without saying a word. Mariah had stepped into his embrace in church, but he was afraid to do or say something that would shatter what felt like such a fragile bond between them.

At their place, Addison said, "I'll put the horses in the shed."

"Leave Percy here. Sally Wilson had a hard delivery. She lost a lot of blood. After I … we get Hope settled, I have to check on her."

No! Another of those thoughts that wanted to shout itself, but restraint sprang from somewhere. She could have said, You abandoned me often enough to go do your duty. She put a hand on his arm. It was too dark to see her expression.

He sighed.

"Maybe I won't have to stay long," she said.

He told himself he'd sighed a sigh of relief, not longing. As soon as that thought coagulated, a flood of emotion burst inside him, and he longed, he ached, he lusted for her.

She patted his arm. "The horses. And a feedbag of oats for Percy."

He stood there as Mariah entered the house and lit a lamp.

Outlaw again nudged his master, and the master waited on the beasts of burden. When he finished, he removed his boots on the side porch and washed his hands. Inside, Mariah sat in the rocker, nursing the baby. She switched Hope from one side to the other. Addison knelt on the floor in front of mother and child, wife, and yes, daughter.

Mariah looked into his eyes, and what passed between them stunned Addison.

She hadn't been in love with him when he proposed marriage. Then she appreciated his selfless act as salvation, saving her and

Hope from shame, and she came to love him for that. Over the ensuing months, there were moments when he'd thought: *She loves me more than she did yesterday.* Those increments of love depth were like things you could measure with a ruler.

What had passed between them through their eyes just then was bottomless.

Mariah extended a hand to him. He took it and rested his other on the back of Hope's head, connecting the three of them, physically, yes, but tying their souls together, through her and his eyes, as well.

The Trinity. He'd just been blessed with a rare moment of spiritual understanding of the God he worshipped. And he knew God was present in that moment of binding.

*****

Mariah stayed all night with Sally Wilson. But she hadn't stayed too long. She'd sensed Sally slipping away a couple of times, and each time, the healer in her encouraged the pale, exhausted woman to dig deeper, to fight, if not for her own life, to fight for her baby.

Sally hadn't wanted anything to eat or drink, but Mariah coaxed her into accepting a few spoonfuls of broth. Shortly after that, she was able to nurse her baby. When her infant was satisfied, Sally took more broth. Then it was time for the healer to address her own mother duties.

Mariah left the Wilson's house and rode Percy down Fourth Street.

A rim of gray haze sat on the horizon, and the sun glowed red through it.

Thank You, Father, for bringing Sally Wilson safely through the night. I'm not sure I could have handled her dying. She smiled. *But, of course, You knew ... know.*

Inside, she found Addison dressing the baby on the changing table. He looked over his shoulder. She expected a smile but got a frown, which engendered one of her own.

"Sally?" he said.

Of course! Addison would be worried about Sally Wilson, but she knew he was more worried about his own wife, the mother of their baby, about Mariah the healer. Had she become Mariah the killer, and lost her curing touch? It squeezed her heart to know how well he understood and how much he cared.

"She made it through the night and was able to nurse her baby this morning."

His frown disintegrated. Then, Hope fussed.

During diaper changes, baths, and getting dressed, the baby endured the activity and was patient. To an extent. She also seemed to have firm ideas about how long such inconveniences should take. Plus, she'd spotted her mother and was hungry again.

While she tended the baby, Addison tended the stove. Aromas of bacon frying and coffee brewing filled the room. Mariah couldn't remember how long it had been since she'd eaten.

There hadn't been time yesterday.

Yesterday! How could a single day contain all that had happened?

It had started with someone pounding on her door at four a.m. The noise woke Hope. *Addison! Somethings happened to him.* That thought stung her heart.

She left the baby crying, turned up the wick on the living room lamp, and answered the door in her nightgown.

"The pains have started," her male visitor blurted. Oscar Wilson. His wife Sally was due to deliver their third child. "I've got my buggy outside. Please hurry."

Mariah invited Oscar inside, returned to her bedroom, and lit another lamp.

"Hurry, please!" came from the living room.

The healer had practice at getting dressed in a hurry. She also had experience in managing priorities in a crisis.

First, she thanked God that her middle-of the-night visitor hadn't come to deliver the most awful news about her husband. Thank You, Lord, for watching over Addison. Please keep him in Your care.

After pulling on her underclothes, she patted Hope and spoke soothing words to her, which caused the baby to rachet up the level of her yowling, which caused her milk to let down.

Mariah slipped into her button-up-the-front dress. She left the top buttons undone and called Oscar to help carry the baby's bag and her medical bag she kept packed.

Outside, a light rain fell. While Oscar drove the buggy, she held an umbrella over herself and the nursed baby.

At the Wilson's house, she found Sally perspiring and grimacing from a contraction. Dora Young, a midwife, and Samantha Ewald, a neighbor, were there as well.

Mariah and the other two women stayed with Sally Wilson all morning, when, at noon, the contractions ceased. The healer and midwife agreed that the baby was probably not coming that day.

The ambush and firing squad both occurred before Sally's contractions started again.

"Breakfast's ready," snapped Mariah back to the present.

Addison took the infant, put a spit up cloth on his shoulder, and began walking and patting his daughter's back. Together, Mariah and he said the before-meal prayer. Hope burped her after meal one.

To Mariah, it seemed like days since she'd had time to eat, to even think about eating. But then, breakfast smells triggered ravenous hunger, and she didn't have time to taste the bacon, eggs, or potatoes. She wolfed down forkful after forkful, barely taking the time to chew.

Addison placed Hope in her basket on the table and sat next to Mariah. He took her hand, not the one with the fork in it.

"Wife," he said.

Utensil hand continued its journey. She chewed, swallowed, dabbed her lips with a napkin, and took a sip of coffee. Then she looked at him and discovered that her soul was much hungrier for the love that poured out of his eyes than her body was for breakfast.

"Wife," he said again. "This is a precious moment, being here with you like this."

Her fork clinked when she placed it on the plate. Looking into his eyes transported her back to their moments of exquisite, intimate, spiritual bonding the night before.

"I feel it, too, Husband. Our love has grown, deepened, and it is forever. It is no longer, 'Til death do us part.'"

That last surprised him. For a moment.

"Wife, our love has grown and deepened, but I feel there is still something between us that keeps us from becoming even closer. I have something I need to tell you about."

"Husband, there are things I need to tell you as well. Our love is forever, though. There is time. Right now, we need to eat. I have to get back to Sally. She made it through last night, and she was able to nurse her baby. Those things are very encouraging, but if we can bring her through today, her survival chances improve tremendously."

Her husband wanted her. Desperately longed for her. Somehow, seeing and knowing of his need made her stronger. Preacher Cromwell's confession from the Penance Pew also made her stronger. She would not have been able to put into words, as he did—and he was still a preacher, a man of God, despite his insistence on the contrary—the soul-troubling emotions killing had stirred in her.

"You're thinking about Preacher Cromwell's confession?"

She nodded.

He quoted: "I was Preacher Cromwell. Then I was Killer Cromwell. Father God, Lord of heaven and earth, please take this killer me away and never give him back. But in this, as in all things, let it be done according to Your will."

"I walked into church just as he sat on the Penance Pew. When he asked for forgiveness, I gave it to him. I do not know where the courage to do that came from. There is more to this that I need to tell you.

"But that is for later.

"We have forever to get it done.

"Right now, we need to eat, and I need to get back to the Wilsons. Their baby needs her mother to abide on earth a bit longer.

"Husband, eat."

He sighed.

But then he ate.

With gusto.

20

Addison put Hope down for a nap. He washed the dishes; then he picked up one of Mariah's books, a volume of Shakespeare's plays, and sat in the rocker, and rocked and read.

Halfway down the page, he recalled Pa giving him a switching if he found his son reading anything other than the Bible. His pa had administered a lot of that kind of punishment for things Addison no longer considered to be a sin. At that time, though, in the Freeman family, Pa's word was the law. He was like a Moses, and he had been entrusted by God with commandments. Except Pa had a lot more than ten of then, too many to put on a stone tablet. Consequently, Addison never knew that what he was doing violated one of Pa's Thou shalt nots until he cut a willow switch.

Addison never argued, never tried to get away. He'd learned such attempted evasions earned him more welts across his back. Ma, too, had learned not to intervene, to beg for mercy for her son. That, too, earned more punishment.

Addison recalled when it had changed between his father and him. It was when the Holy Crusade wagon train passed through Thompson Township, Illinois. The mayor and sheriff of the town both bore the same last name, Thompson. The mayor was especially rabid in his anti-abolitionist sentiment. In an altercation, the Crusaders managed to get the upper hand, and they locked the mayor, the sheriff, and some of their henchmen in the jail. When the prisoners tried to escape, Addison had been forced to shoot and kill three of them.

It had taken some talking from Joshua Reedley to accept what he'd done, shoot those men dead, but after that, he never accepted a switching from his Pa again.

From that point on, Addison made up his own mind about the right and wrong of things. Even though he'd thought, in some ways, it was easier to just let his pa do that for him. In some ways, it was easier to just accept an unjustified switching than to have make weighty moral decisions all on his own.

That thought transported him from Thompson Township, Illinois, back to Brotherton, Kansas. He looked down at the open book in his lap but did not see words on the page.

Addison raised his head and closed his eyes. It was easier to see heaven that way.

Father in heaven, please touch the Wilson woman with your healing hand. You know better than me, if that woman dies, Mariah will carry her life on her soul as a greater burden than the man she shot as part of the firing squad.

There was a knock.

He closed the book, hurried to and opened the door.

Maybell Jim stood on the porch. "Is Mariah here?"

Addison shook his head. "She's with Sally Wilson."

"Marshal McTavish tole me to fetch the two of you to the Meetin' House."

"Hope's sleeping. Could you—"

"Cain't. I gots to be dere, too." Maybell frowned and trotted the sentence out again. "I have to be there, too. Bring the baby. Where do the Wilsons live?"

"Fourth Street. Coupla houses west of C. On the left side."

Maybell spun on her heel, stepped off the porch, and swung up onto the saddle of her ground-hitched gray.

He went into the bedroom and woke the baby.

Another of Hope's well-formed convictions: It was her job to wake people. It wasn't supposed to work the other way. She cried when he woke her, cried as he arranged her in her basket, and cried along the whole eastern half of Main Street.

Ma waited outside the Meeting House. "I'll take her." She lifted the little noise maker and cooed soft words. Hope stopped wailing, studied her grandmother's face, and snuffed in two short, sharp inhales as if to make up for all the air expended in protesting the disturbance of her sleep.

"They're waiting for you in there," Ma said.

Addison watched cooing Grandma walk away with her silent grandchild, for a moment, before shaking his head and stepping inside.

Marshal McTavish, Joshua Reedley, Mayor Argyl, and Preacher Larrimer sat behind a table facing Jibway and another man in the middle of the first row of chairs. Two others lay on blankets on the floor. These appeared to be unconscious. Both wore blood-stained shirts.

Mariah and Maybell entered the hall from the kitchen.

Addison watched his wife, the healer, stop and take in the scene. She cast him the briefest glance. Then she strode toward the prostrate men and knelt beside one. She felt for a pulse, placed her hand on the man's chest, and shook her head.

Addison didn't have to be a healer to see the other man's chest rise and fall.

Mariah knelt beside this one and peeled back his bloody shirt. Someone had tied a leather strap holding a folded cloth soaked with blood to the left side of the chest.

"Maybell, you said you could hear air whistle in and out of the bullet hole?"

"We could. Jibway put that bandage on."

"You saved his life," Mariah said to Jibway. "I'd like him moved to the cot in my office. We need to make sure the wound is clean so an infection won't set in."

The marshal sent his son, Charlie, to roust up some help.

Preacher Larrimer moved around the table and knelt next to the deceased bushwhacker. He asked the Lord to forgive the man of his sins and to accept his soul into heaven.

As the preacher rose to his feet, Charlie returned with four men. Two of them moved the wounded man to Mariah's office. The other two carried the deceased to a rear corner of the hall.

The marshal thanked them, dismissal clear as day in his words.

When the front door closed, Preacher Larrimer said, "Who's that next to you, Jibway?"

Jibway elbowed the man.

"I'm Rob Batchelder."

"And you promised to not bear arms against us ever again. That right?" the marshal said.

"Yes, sir. That's the truth."

McTavish said, "Now, Jibway, tell us what happened."

Jibway nodded. "Maybell and I decided—"

"You decided, or Maybell decided?"

"We decided, Marshal," Maybell said and sat next to her husband. "Some of the pro-slaver gang of murderers escaped from our ambush. We wanted to make sure those runaways, plus the ones put on parole, didn't meet up and sneak back and attack us again."

"A goodly number of the men in that raiding party had been given a parole before," Jibway said. "They broke their promises. We thought it prudent to make sure a promise meant something to the twelve newest names in your parole ledger."

"Prudent," Maybell said like an exclamation point on her husband's words.

Jibway and Maybell had trailed the dozen. Half of the group were wounded. All of them were dispirited.

"We trailed them from a distance," Maybell said. "They was … were easy to track with Jibway's binoculars. Just before sundown, the group came upon a horse just standing there on the prairie. Jibway thought a man was on the ground close to it. Probably wounded. The ones we followed dismounted. We did, too, and walked close to our mounts, so if they saw us, they'd think we were just a couple of stray horses from the ambush."

Jibway reported, "It wasn't long before they lit a fire, with the kindling we strapped behind one of their saddles. We moved closer."

Maybell took over. "Then Jibway made me wait with the horses. He said I make as much noise as a white man when I'm trying to be quiet."

Marshal McTavish cleared his throat.

Jibway again, "I got close enough to hear them talking. There was a man on the ground. He had a busted arm and leg." He nudged the man next to him again.

Wesley? Addison wondered.

"His name was Wesley Crane," Batchelder said. "Wesley said an abolitionist shot him in the arm. A little later, Wesley's horse got shot and fell on his leg. The abolitionist splinted up his broken bones and gave him another horse. Wesley said he rode to that spot where he met up with our raidin' party. Mort, he was our leader, told Wes they'd find him again after we burned Brotherton."

Joshua Reedley looked at Addison. "You patched up that Wesley?"

"Yes, sir."

"Why?" Marshal McTavish blurted.

Addison said, "He wasn't a parole breaker."

McTavish fired, "How'd you know that?"

"I just figured he wasn't."

"You figured?"

"He figures things pretty good," Reedley said and nodded to Addison, which he figured meant sit down. So, he did. Next to Maybell.

"Jibway, what happened next?" the marshal said.

"About the time I first smelled coffee, a voice hailed the camp. One of the paroled, Yancey Clinton, hollered, 'Who's out there?' 'Val Manson,' came the reply.

"Another one of the paroled said, 'Val Manson! As soon as the shootin' started at the ambush, he turned tail and ran.'"

Jibway described a jumbled conversation in which some at the campfire wanted to let Manson join them, but others wanted to tell him to "go the hell away." Yancey Clinton, though, decided they should invite the man to join them. Which Yancey did. They then gave Manson a cup of coffee and something to eat.

"Tell them what happened next," Jibway said to Batchelder.

"After he et, Manson said he was going to Brotherton and start shooting abolitionists. Val had a buffler' gun, an' he could hit a target from a long ways off. He wanted one of us to go with him. Be his spotter. Watch for people sneaking up on him as he lined up targets."

"Rob here," Jibway said, "told Manson they had all promised not to bear arms against free-staters ever again. Manson shot back with, 'Promise to a abolitionist don't mean nothing.' Wesley Crane said, 'If our promises don't mean nothin', we don't mean nothin' neither, Val.'"

Batchelder said, "We had an argument. Four, with their brand-new paroles, wanted to go with Manson. I said, 'None of us could go with him. We all promised.' Next thing we heard, 'Ain't nobody stoppin' me. I'm going with him.' 'Me, too.' Pistols was drawn. A shot was fired. Then all hell broke loose. Manson leveled that cannon a his at me, but I shot him first. Then I flopped to the ground. Quick as it started, it stopped quick, too."

"Wesley?"

Batchelder looked at Addison and shook his head. "Before Manson showed up, Wesley said he'd asked you why you patched him up. You said one day we'd be livin' together here in Kansas and not shootin' at each other no more. You said you needed to practice how to get along with folks you used to shoot at."

Every eye at the inquisitor table stared at Addison. Mariah stood outside her corner office. She stared, too. From outside the hall, sounds of horses. Wagons, and muted voices penetrated the walls of the building. Inside, it was tomb silent. It was as if Addison heard those outside noises like he was dreaming, like those weren't real-world sounds.

Preacher Larrimer broke eye contact with Addison. The wispiest ghost of a smile tried like heck to climb onto the preacher's face, and almost made it.

"Maybell," Larrimer said. "Would you be kind enough to fetch Preacher Cromwell, please?"

Maybell departed on her errand.

Batchelder reported the rest of the story to the inquisitors: Manson, Wesley Crane, and four others had been killed at the campfire gunfight. The dead were buried there. Five of the paroled men continued toward their homes. Jibway and Maybell rigged travois to bring the one wounded and one now deceased back to Brotherton.

Batchelder asked Jibway if he could come back to Brotherton, too. He said he thought he should practice trying to get along with abolitionists he used to shoot at. "Who knows. With enough practice, even a dunce like me might learn how to do just that."

Preacher Larrimer announced that the funeral for Sean O'Riley and Eileen Nelson would be set back to eleven a.m.

Bob Batchelder helped Joshua Reedley update the Parole Ledger.

Mariah treated the wounded man, Ezra Egan. Then, she visited her mother-in-law and daughter before checking on Sally Wilson and returning in time for the funeral.

Marshal McTavish, Joshua Reedley, Addison, and Jibway conferred on how to protect Brotherton from threats such as Val Manson would have posed. They decided to form four teams to scout the perimeters of Brotherton along the four sides of the town, specifically searching for possible long-range shooter hideouts. They'd begin the search as soon as the funeral ended.

"One more thing," the marshal said. "We've got to deal with our two pro-slavery prisoners. Any ideas?"

Addison said, "Right before you called this meeting, I heard Batchelder and the wounded man, Ezra Egan, in Mariah's office. They both said they were not pro-slavery, they were pro-state's-rights. 'Think about it,' Batchelder said to Egan, 'they're fighting for the right of Kansas to determine how it will enter the Union. They're fightin' for the same thing we are!'

"Then Ezra said he sure never saw it that way.

"And Batchelder said, 'Plus, they seem to be honest men. They give a promise, they keep it. Not like that passel of forked-tongue devils we throwed in with. I'm gonna ask to stay with them.' And Egan said, 'Ask for me, too.'"

"Deciding that sounds like a job for the mayor and Preacher Larrimer," Reedley said.

McTavish nodded. "Right now, though, we got a double funeral to attend."

*****

After the graveside services concluded, Addison took Rob Batchelder with him to scout along the northern boundary of the town. Up there, it was all open prairie, fields, and pastures. Not much place for a shooter to hide.

Addison remembered how he, and even Outlaw, had hidden in the prairie grass to ambush pro-slavers. "Lots of one and two-person plowing, planting, and harvesting goes on up here," he said to Batchelder.

"A shooter could sneak in at night, hunker down in the grass, and when farmers showed up, he could pick them off and skedaddle afore anyone got here," Rob pointed out.

They rode at a walk, side-by-side, headed away from the late day sun.

"Seems funny," Batchelder said. "A day or so ago, we was enemies. And the men I rode with made empty promises. But here you are a trustin' me."

"Jibway Jim taught me a lot about reading sign."

"So, you read me as someone you can trust?"

"I trust you." After Outlaw's head bobbed twice, he added, "Some."

Batchelder bobbed his own head twice.

21

Addison made it home just after dark. A lamp glowed warmth and welcome through the front window.

Please, God, let it be Mariah, not Ma.

Uh, no offense, Ma.

He opened the door. The smell of supper and the sight of Mariah in the rocker, a book in her hands, greeted him.

Addison got one foot inside when she ran into his arms. They hugged. They kissed. They hugged some more.

"We should close the door," he said.

She kissed him again.

When he was able, he moved her and himself far enough to kick the door closed. Somehow, along with other thoughts rampaging frantically through his brain, worry over a long-range shooter had urged him to seal off the outside. But he didn't say anything. He didn't want to worry her.

"You're worried about a buffalo gun."

"So, Mariah the healer," he said, "now you're Mariah the mind reader?"

Her perfectly serious face pronounced, "I can only read yours." Then, a cloud of real seriousness dimmed the brightness of her manufactured sunshine. "I confess. Maybell told me about the man they found, the one who wanted to shoot us down from a long way off. Plus, I have a new understanding of what you do to keep the rest of us safe. You and Joshua Reedley and Jibway and Marshal McTavish. I took what you did for granted and was only annoyed at being separated from you."

He thought It was funny. A mere moment ago, no power on earth could have prevented him from picking up Mariah and carrying her to the bedroom. But then she'd mentioned the buffalo gun. If she hadn't said what she did, his concern for that particular threat would have evaporated when he got the door closed. "Buffalo gun," however, forced him to acknowledge that even in the heat of passion, some part of his awareness probed for danger.

Thank You, Father God, for planting this ability in my feeble brain.

With passion at bay for the moment, sort of like O'Riley's wolfhound on a leash, he wondered if Mariah would talk to him about being behind the barricade and in the firing squad. He knew she wanted to talk to him about those experiences.

She did want to talk, it turned out, but not about those subjects. At least not then. As she tended Hope and he dished up supper, she rattled on about her patients and friends and his mother as if silence were abhorrent.

When they sat at the table, Addison said the before-meal prayer.

Then Mariah took a dainty forkful, chewed, swallowed, and began again to fill the kitchen with words. As he ate, Addison watched Mariah. It was as if she got more nourishment from pouring words out of her mouth than putting food into it.

Females. The most wondrous creatures in all of creation. If God had created Eve first, He would not have seen the need for an Adam. I'll have to tell her that. If I can get a word in edgewise.

"What are you smirking about?" Her question jerked him abruptly from sublimity.

"Um," he said. "Suppers finished. Why don't you get Hope ready for bed? I'll wash the dishes."

She regarded him, silently, for a moment. Then she rose and did as he suggested.

*****

As Mariah donned her nightgown, she thought, *Finally*. That night, finally, it was the right time to tell Addison about being behind the barricade. And in the firing squad. Before, her duties as a healer got in the way. But, too, her thoughts had been so jumbled, she hadn't known how to even start the telling. Now, though, there was an urgency to extract the confession stuck in her soul like a diseased tooth.

As she slipped under the covers, Mariah prayed that Hope would permit her parents the minutes they needed. Normally, when they went to bed, they extinguished the lamp in their bedroom and left the door open. Enough light spilled in from the living room lamp to tend the baby. That night, Mariah told Addison to leave the bedside lamp lit.

He got in bed. She was on her side. He turned onto his.

She caressed his face. He'd shaved. Funny. Tonight, if your whiskers scratched my face bloody, I wouldn't mind. "It seems like—"

"Forever," he supplied. "You talked about forever. Remember?"

"Yes, but I never expected to have to use it to describe how long it's been since we lay together like this."

"So tonight, forever ends." He took her hand from his face and kissed it. "The way forever works, when a forever ends, another begins immed—"

Her kiss shut him up. Which woke ardor.

She pushed him back. Somewhat effectively.

"There's something I have to tell you." He ceased pulling her toward him.

She told him about being behind the barricade. How, before the shooting started, all she did was wonder whatever possessed her to want to be there with a long gun in her hands and waiting to shoot a man, or men.

"And the waiting got to be so horrible. At first, I reminded myself of the terrible things some of the pro-slavers wanted to do to us on earlier raids. Kill us all, even Hope, and scalp us and receive a bounty for each one they took. Those thoughts lasted but a moment. Then I began wondering what Mariah, the Healer, was doing there. I thought I wanted to know what it was like to do what you did to protect us, but then I thought about throwing the gun away from me and laying on the ground with my hands over my ears and eyes shut and holding my breath. I didn't even want air from the world outside me to breathe. But the woman next to me was so calm, some of it spilled over and into me."

Mariah took a deep breath and let it out. Addison was looking at her, with love, with compassion. With understanding.

"You felt like that once, too?" she said.

He explained about killing three men near the start of Found Grace Church's Holy Crusade. "But I would never have been able to be part of a firing squad immediately after that experience."

Mariah'd had the notion that killing people was easier for men than for women. Addison said that was not the case. There was something comforting in that idea. She frowned, annoyance with herself supplanting comfort from him. She'd sidetracked the conversation when her story wanted so desperately to be told.

She said, "Just before the shooting began, I realized that all of those behind the barricades were there to protect, first, me and the rest of us out there, and second to protect all Brotherton. I owed the others behind the barricades my best effort to protect them as they were fighting to protect me."

Addison nodded, but more than the nod, his eyes poured understanding into hers. His understanding meant so much, filled her heart with such affection for him, she almost pulled him to her. But she had one more thing she wanted to say to him.

"After the first wave of shooting died out, Eileen Nelson, who was next to me, stood up, and she was killed. I felt as if I had let Eileen down, like I hadn't protected her after she poured some of her courage into me. And then, they shot Sean O'Riley, too. When the marshal asked for volunteers for the firing squad, I had to do it. I couldn't let anyone else bear that burden for me. Do you understand?"

"I do," he said in his don't-wake-the-baby whisper.

She grabbed his shoulder to pull him to her, but he held back. "I have something to tell you, too."

He told her about how he'd found it impossible to execute parole breakers, to shoot those unarmed men in cold blood, no matter what they'd done, and how Jibway had done it for him. But, Jibway hadn't been there when he encountered three-time parole-breaker Abel Conway and had to shoot him.

"Wife, thank you." He searched for more words to say, to confess, to share with her, but none came.

"Husband, do you not see the fingerprints of God in all this? Say a prayer. Thank Him."

He voiced thanks to God out loud quietly.

Then they came together, and it was wedding night sacred.

*****

Addison and Timothy O'Riley sat facing Marshal McTavish behind his desk in his new office on Seventh Street. It was the first Monday in the November. The door stood open to the unseasonably pleasant air outside. The three men were discussing the possibility of using O'Riley's wolfhound with the long-range-shooter scouting parties.

"I don't know," Timothy said. "Our patrols reduce the odds that a shooter can get into position to pick us off, but there's still a chance a clever devil will sneak into a hidey hole. If he does and sees us coming with a dog, was it me, I'd shoot the dog first, then the men."

"Winds here are normally from the west," Addison said. "Jibway's horse, and mine, are good at smelling trouble as long as they are heading into the wind. I thought your hound would be even better."

"Our scouts are risking their necks to protect us against a long gun, O'Riley," McTavish said. "Are you saying your dog is worth more than a man or a woman?"

Timothy's chin jutted forward. "Worth just as much!"

McTavish sputtered. "Irishman."

"Scotsman!" Timothy fired back.

"This is how I think we should do it," Addison piped in. "The greatest risk is along the Delaware River. More places to hide there, and the area to the north is almost as good for a shooter to hunker down. We should take turns scouting east and north. Jibway and his horse, me and mine, Joshua Reedley, and Mr. O'Riley and his hound. We should start at the ferry crossing and ride north along the river until we get above Eighth Street, then cut west."

O'Riley's head snapped to the side, and he aimed his glower at Addison. "Take turns, you said. You want Hound and me to be looking for pro-slavery skulkers all day every day?"

"That's not what he means, Timothy," the marshal said. "That's not what you meant, right, Addison?"

"Right, Marshal. Jibway would lead the patrol one day. I'd do the second. We'd want Mr. O'Riley and Hound every third day. We figured the best chance the pro-slavers would slip by our normal patrols is in the middle of the night. What we'd want Mr. O'Riley to do is to team up with another man or woman, start at the ferry crossing two hours before sunup, and patrol north, then cut west. If anyone gets some inclination a pro-slaver is hiding ahead of us, we stop and send the other scout to get help. If Mr. O'Riley and Hound don't find a shooter, their patrol would be over in three or four hours."

The Irishman faced the Scotsman again. "Potts, at the trading post, says we'll get snow by the end of the week. Once we get snow on the ground, we shouldn't have to worry about the pro-slavers."

"Ach!" the marshal said. "Potts and his rheumatism predicting the weather! But we talked about this in Town Council. The pro-slavers are a determined bunch of devils. They were not able to get at us coming from the south and the east, so they tried to sneak around and attack us from the west. Fortunately, with the good Lord's help, we were able to stop them. They are not just going to stop trying to kill us. So, we need to remain vigilant, even in winter, even with snow on the ground. We need your help, Timothy. Yours and your hound's."

That arrow, Addison saw, penetrated the Irishman's armor.

A rider pulled up outside the office, dismounted, and entered. He removed his hat. It was a young man from Preacher Cromwell's group. "Mr. Reedley sent me. He said to tell you the latest Emigrant Aid Society wagon train of east coasters is at the ferry landing."

Marshal McTavish thanked the messenger, and he thanked Timothy O'Riley for agreeing to help with the long-range-shooter patrols.

Addison almost smiled. O'Riley's jaw muscles worked as if he were chewing on the notion tthat he'd allowed the Scotsman to bamboozle him into doing something he did not want to do.

"Let's go greet our new neighbors," the marshal said.

Addison and Scout followed the older men down B Street to the lot behind the Meeting House, where they left their horses.

On the other side of the Meeting House, the people of Brotherton lined both sides of Main Street to welcome the newcomers. Most of the young bachelors, including Orson Seiling, stood on the dirt in front of the boardwalk. They also wanted to welcome the east coasters, and to examine some of them. These young men, Addison noted, cared not a whit for the men, married women, or children. They had eyes only for the young ladies.

Addison had never before been able to stand and watch newcomer wagons enter town. He'd always been with the wagon train, serving as a scout. Now, watching the bachelors, he smiled, until he wondered if he'd somehow gotten old.

Jibway was in the lead. He turned right down C Street.

Next to the second wagon, a young blonde, attired in pants, wearing a man's hat above her shoulder-length hair, rode a chestnut mare. She stared straight ahead as if she didn't notice the attention directed at her.

Jibway, leading, turned right down C Street. The wagons and Miss Pants followed. Orson's boots stomping on the boardwalk in front of the Meeting House triggered a stampede after him.

Joshua Reedley grabbed Addison's arm and invited him inside the Meeting House. Marshal McTavish wanted to hear how the scouting party had performed. Reedley had promoted the idea of having Jibway act as lead and using several of the younger and less experienced men and women to help him. The marshal had not been enthusiastic about Reedley's idea. He'd voiced concern not only over the lack of experience, and the idea of sending, "Married couples as scouts?"

Jibway's party included Maybell Jim, Charlie McTavish, Maurice Reedley, and his wife Eunice.

Inside the Meeting House, Marshal McTavish sat behind a table facing Reedley, Addison, Jibway, and his son Charlie, seated on first-row chairs.

"How'd this *scouting*—the marshal's disdain dripped from the word—party do, Charlie?"

"Well, uh—"

Jibway stood. "Marshal, in general, the group performed well. Yesterday morning, Maybell and your boy scouted ahead and to the south of us. They picked up sign, followed it, and found where four men had hidden. The four skedaddled, but Maybell rode one down and knocked him from his horse. Turns out, these men had intended on sneaking into our camp last night and stealing from us."

The marshal stared at his son for a long, uncomfortable moment; then he said, "So, this man that Maybell unhorsed, he was a little guy?"

Jibway said, "Tell him, Charlie."

"Not little. He was big as Hermann Vogelsang. Maybell rode to alongside him and smacked him in the face with her pistol. He tumbled from the saddle. She reined up, hopped down, rolled the thief onto his belly, knelt on his back, and tied his hands behind him."

"What'd you do to the thief?" the marshal asked Jibway.

"I cut a notch out of his left ear." Jibway said. "Told him if I caught him trying to rob anyone ever again, I'd cut his nose off. Then I let him go. He rode east."

The marshal's meeting broke up, and the others left. Reedley and Addison stayed.

"Addison, take Charlie under your wing. You turned Orson Seiling around. You ought to be able to make a scout out of Charlie."

"Mr. Reedley—"

"I know. You had him with you during the last pro-slavery raid. But it took you months to make a man of Orson."

"Mr. Reedley—"

Joshua glared at Addison. The glare said: Time for talking is done. Time for doing is here.

1860

On Saturday, January 14th, Otto Vogelsang oversaw the installation of the preacher's and deacon's podiums in Brotherton's second house of worship on Eighth Street. The next day, Preacher Larrimer opened the first church service with a Rite of Ordination for Caleb Cromwell.

Larrimer had argued against such a procedure, because, first, he was not a bishop, and second, Preacher Cromwell's consecration to the ministry had never been set aside.

Cromwell pleaded for the service. "My experiences last fall so changed me, no part of me is the same as when I first pledged myself to serve the Lord."

Preacher Larrimer conducted the reordination.

From the second to last row of pews, Addison watched his stern-visaged preacher reconsecrate Caleb Cromwell to the service of God the Father. No hint of emotion seeped onto Preacher Larrimer's stone face, but Addison knew he was not the same man who launched the Holy Crusade almost two years prior. He wasn't seeing the transformation. Rather, he felt it.

Mariah squeezed his hand. She feels something, too. He looked at her.

Since the day of the barricades, each night in bed, they shared the thoughts, the feelings, the questions they'd experienced during the day. Eyes were said to be the windows to the soul. But, through their whispered words, they bared their spiritual beings to each other.

Preacher Larrimer recaptured their attention. "Rise, Caleb Cromwell, ordained minister of The Word."

Larrimer left the podium to sit next to his wife on a first-row pew.

Preacher Cromwell walked behind the altar and consecrated it. He consecrated the penance pew and the entire building to the service of The Creator as The Church of God Most Holy.

*****

On the night of January 15, it snowed six inches. At ten o'clock the next morning, Preacher Cromwell joined Orson Seiling and Miss Pants, Christian name, Lorelei Belmont, in holy matrimony in The Church of God Most Holy.

Lorelei wore a dress as dazzlingly white as the sun on the snow outside.

Addison J. Freeman served as best man.

*****

That night, Mariah checked on Hope before coming to bed. They'd moved the baby to the second bedroom at the start of the new year.

As she slipped beneath the covers, Mariah posited, still using her don't-wake-the-baby whisper, "Hope likes this new arrangement."

"Of course," he whisper replied, "She doesn't have to listen to us blabbermouth all night."

"You mean have heartfelt conversation?"

"Heartfelt conversation. That's what I meant to say."

He kissed her, and she kissed back, for a moment.

"Lorelei's dress," Mariah said. "Her mother sewed it for her from material they brought from the east coast. That dress is only intended to be worn at the wedding and never again. Though Lorelei told me, she intends to wear it on her tenth wedding anniversary. 'Aiming for that will keep me from getting fat like most wives do,' she said.

Then she hastened to add that I hadn't gotten fat, though I was sure in her mind she appended a *yet* onto her spoken words."

"A dress to be worn only once, or even twice, seems sinfully wasteful. Are the Belmonts that rich?"

"They had Ziggy Hostetler deliver wine to serve at the reception in the Meeting House."

"That makes them richer than we are." Addison paused. "In a way that counts for nothing in the eyes of God. In His eyes, and in mine, He has made me the richest man in the world."

In Mariah's breast, passion flared like a coal-oil-soaked log on the hearth after coming home to a cold, cold house at the end of long, long day. She forestalled it. One other item needed to be discussed.

"Addison." She squeezed his hand. "At the reception, after the wedding, when Orson toasted you before you could toast him and his bride, I couldn't tell if you were surprised or not. Were you? Surprised?"

"Yes. And no." The lit bedside lamp was behind her husband, so she couldn't see the expression on his face. "You know Orson's Ma asked Reedley to take her son under his wing, to straighten him out, to make a man of him. Joshua passed the job to me. Almost two years ago."

Mariah lay beside him, afraid to move, fearing she'd disturb that delicate assembly of emotions permitting her husband to speak about her former lover.

"Make a man of Orson Seiling." Bitterness tinged his words. "Make a man out of a kid who refused to grow up. I tried to talk to him, tried to point out to him the things he did wrong, but he wouldn't listen. I started hitting him, trying to get him to pay attention to what I was telling him. But he would not listen. So, I stopped trying to talk to him and started hitting him when I saw him … misbehave."

Mariah's heart pumped a spurt of fear into her veins. Is he going to talk about me and Orson next?

"Hitting him didn't work any better than talking to him. He never tried to hit me back, never even tried to block my punches. His cunning little brain figured out that was the best way to get me to stop hitting him. I stopped, ready to tell Joshua Reedley that if there was a man inside Orson, I was incapable of digging him, or it, out."

Another pause, as if Addison's mind were catching its breath.

Mine needs to catch its breath, too.

Addison exhaled a gentle sigh. "Remember when the pro-slavers attacked us, intending to kill us all, scalp us, and sell our bloody hair to the sheriff in Prairietown?" He didn't wait for an answer. "We went down there, and one of the things we found was how the sheriff treated his female slaves. He allowed the scalp takers to use them. Orson saw that, and it got to him in a way my fists never could. Orson never told me it did, but after that, he began to change.

"At the wedding reception, Orson gave me all the credit for making him see 'the error of his ways.' But it was really him seeing the example of that grievous sin that changed him."

"Husband, I am sure that without you being stern and forceful with Orson, he'd have missed the example The Lord set before him, and he'd still be going through life relying on his charm and good looks to get what he wants."

She kissed him. "Orson was right. You really are the best, best man."

Hope was beginning to sleep through the night. It didn't always happen that way, but that night, it did. Mariah was especially grateful and stayed awake until Addison's hand holding hers relaxed.

God most holy, thank You for this best, best husband You have blessed me with. Thank You, that he never brings up Orson and me. Thank You for our best, best baby. Amen.

As she began to slip beneath the surface of the lake of sleep, a thought, framed with a bit of worry-rust, tried to stay her descent, but it failed.

*****

After supper and dessert, Addison sipped coffee. Next to him, Mariah poured a cup for herself. Hope, in her basket on the table, played with a rattle toy Maybell had made. Father took Mother's hand.

"Wife," he whispered, which elicited a smile. When it was just the three of them in the house, Addison and Mariah had adopted their don't-wake-the-baby voices as their normal way to speak with each other. Even if, as then, Hope was wide awake. They both thought it was odd, but neither wanted to change.

"It occurred to me," he said, "that this winter, our lives have settled into what we might call normal. For me, ever since we left Illinois two years ago, there has been no normal. Every single day was filled with experiences I'd never had before and could not even imagine. But this winter, it seems like I returned to what life on our farm was like."

"Without the switchings from your pa."

"Well, yes, without those."

"And you were in love with Lizbeth then."

Addison frowned, and Mariah giggled. "Sorry," she said, though she didn't look sorry.

They spoke then about the kind of living that had visited Brotherton that winter. Addison had mended harnesses and machinery, had done stints feeding livestock in the communal barn, stood watches in the town marshal's office, gone on long-range shooter patrols, attended church services, and, except for the two times he'd been away for four days while scouting for a Ziggy Hostetler supply wagon train, he'd been home for supper each night.

Mariah recounted dealing with cuts, bruises, a few broken bones, whooping cough, colic, a baby who wouldn't nurse, but no bullet wounds. She also mentioned attending services with Preacher Cromwell on alternate weeks.

"Wife, I never appreciated normal back in Illinois, but I sure do here."

"Husband, you're speaking of nice normal. The normal we had last year the newspapers called Bleeding Kansas."

"And you said our normal was full of bullet holes."

They turned a conjoined gaze of parental pride and wonder on their one-year-old.

"Hopefully," Addison said, and Mariah elbowed him in the ribs. He rubbed the spot. "Hopefully," pausing to see if his ribs would be assaulted again, "you, dearest daughter, will grow up in a nice normal."

*****

Addison, Jibway, Charlie McTavish, Joshua Reedley, Marshal McTavish, and Mayor Gallant Argyl sat around a table in the Meeting House drinking coffee.

"I just returned from the trading post," the mayor said. "Mr. Potts told me it's not unusual for it to snow in March, but thirteen inches of snow overnight is."

"It's what we have to deal with," Reedley said. "If a pro-slaver got into position last night any time before the snow stopped falling, there'd be no sign of him. He could kill both men of our long-range-shooter patrol before they could get away."

"What are the odds a pro-slaver would happen into a good ambush spot just before it snowed?" the mayor said.

"The odds don't matter," Reedley said. "It's possible. That matters."

Reedley laid out a plan to deal with the possible. He'd acquired a dozen long-range guns. In practice, Orson Seiling and Maurice Reedley proved to be the best marksmen. Orson would be placed in the bell tower of New Found Grace Church with a spotter with a long glass. Maurice and a spotter would be stationed in the belltower of The Church of God Most Holy. The long-range-shooter patrols would be doubled to four men each.

Addison and Charlie McTavish, along with Jibway and Maybell Jim, were assigned to the patrol the route along the west bank of the Delaware River and then north of town.

Jibway led. Maybell trailed him. Addison trailed her. Charlie came last. Each of them led a spare horse. Plowing through the deep snow would tire their mounts, so they planned to switch saddles often.

Jibway led them north clear of the saplings, trees and brush covering the bank of the Delaware. His horse plowed a trail for the others to follow.

Addison checked the sun. It was about nine. Usually, they started the patrol earlier, but they'd had to figure out how to cope with the snow. The marshal and the mayor did not think they needed to mount the patrols that morning. Joshua and Jibway thought they did. Addison agreed with the latter two.

The temperature was in the low twenty-degree range. A thin glaze of ice covered the snow. Reedley had insisted they all tie canvas around the horses' lower forelegs. Without the horse boots, the legs on Jibway's mount would be bloody by now. Ahead of him, Jibway and Maybell expelled clouds of breath. The sun, devoid of warmth, hung in the blue sky and shed icy glitter on the snow. Addison flexed his fingers and rubbed his gloved hands together, trying to keep his fingers from stiffening. He checked to the rear.

Charlie was hunkered over, not watching, and falling behind. Addison hollered at him to pay attention and keep up. He didn't react. *Is he sleeping?*

Addison wheeled around, rode next to Charlie, and shoved him out of the saddle.

Charlie lay on his back flailing his arms like an upside-down turtle. His hat lay next to him.

"The hell d'jou do that for?"

Jibway reined up. "The hell d'jou do that for?"

Addison frowned. Was mimicking the McTavish kid supposed to be a joke?

"He be Injun," Jibway said, "We take his clothes and horse. Leave him for buzzards. They come eat him before he freeze solid. They eat him while he still alive. People in Atchison hear him scream."

Maybell joined the gaggle, hopped down, grabbed a handful of snow, and rubbed it over Charlie's face.

"Stop, you black bitch!"

Maybell stopped.

Addison thought the world stopped. For a moment. He started to dismount, but Jibway grabbed his arm.

"Oh, Ize so sorry, Massa Charlie." Maybell oozed servility. "Lemme hep you up."

He pushed her hand away and sat up.

She pulled the collar of his coat back and stuffed another handful of snow inside.

He yowled, cursed, and swung at her.

She parried with her right and shot a left jab at his nose.

He yowled again and raised his hands to his face. Bright red blood oozed through his gloved fingers and dripped onto his lap.

Charlie lowered his hands and regarded the blood. He glared at Maybell and struggled to his feet.

Hit him now. Addison hoped the thought would transport itself to Maybell. Once Charlie got to his feet, his size, weight, and reach advantages would result in a severe beating. Addison started to dismount again. Again, Jibway stopped him.

Charlie glowered hate and murder at the small woman before him. He launched a looping right roundhouse. Addison thought the punch would fling Maybell ten or even fifteen feet. He thought it might kill her.

Maybell leaned over, and the fist sailed over her head as she kicked his right knee, then jumped aside as he fell like an oak destined for the sawmill.

The new yowl from Charlie might have been heard in Atchison with a little help from the prevailing westerlies, but these were frozen dead, too.

Charlie's holler subsided into a moan. He held his knee and rocked back and forth.

"White Man," Jibway said. "I be you, I stop fightin' afore I gits myself crippled up like that Titus lives wit us back in Brotherton."

After Otto Vogelsang had gotten a good start building Brotherton, the pro-slavers mounted a raid intent on killing the Holy Crusaders and receiving a bounty for their scalps from the sheriff in Prairietown. The Crusaders fought off the scalpers and attacked the sheriff's farm.

One of the sheriff's men, Titus, was wounded in the battle and would never walk again. The Crusaders brought him back with them to Brotherton. Otto Vogelsang built him a wheeled chair. Though he was confined to the chair, he'd found a way to earn a living. He kept records for the town of Brotherton and a business that had partnered with Ziggy Hostetler in supplying merchants in Prairietown and Lawrence with goods.

"So, here's how things lay, Charlie," Addison said. "First choice you have to make: are you going to fight with Maybell anymore? Before you decide, remember Titus."

"You gonna tell anybody I got beat up by a girl?"

"No, Charlie," Addison said. "You're going to tell them from the penance pew."

Charlie swore.

"And you can confess cussing, too."

Charlie sat up and grimaced, probably from his bunged-up leg, Addison thought. Or maybe the threat of the penance pew.

"Second thing, you want to ride with us or go back?"

"If I want to go back, you gonna make me walk?"

"You decide, Maybell."

"We won't make you walk. You can keep your horse. Ride to the nearest house this side of town, warm up, then go back to your daddy."

Charlie's rosy cheeks flared crimson. He started raising a gloved hand to his nose, thought better of it, and looked up at Addison.

"Ride with," Charlie said.

"Ride with," Addison repeated. "You got any idea what that means to Maybell, Jibway, and me?"

Charlie shook his head. "Right now, I don't, but by the end of the day, I'll know more than I do now. Assuming, of course, Maybell doesn't feed me to Jibway's vultures."

Maybell pulled off a glove and said, "Open your mouth, Charlie." He did, and she stuck the glove in, and said, "Bite down." He bit, and she straightened his nose. He grunted, removed the glove from his mouth, and wiped the bloody slobber on his pants leg. "Sorry," he said. "And I'm sorry for what I called you earlier."

Maybell stuck out her hand, planted her feet, and hauled Charlie to his. Then she helped him hobble to his horse, and supported his right side while he got his left boot in the stirrup and pulled himself up onto the saddle.

"We ready now to look for a long-rang-shooter?" Jibway said.

"I'm," Charlie stopped. "We're ready."

Jibway headed off north. Maybell followed him. Charlie tagged on after her.

"The Lord works in mysterious ways," Addison said.

Outlaw bobbed his head.

"And please, Lord, help Charlie learn his lessons without getting his fool self killed."

Outlaw snorted.

Addison stopped to switch Charlie and himself to their spare horses. Before they mounted, he had Charlie remove his gloves and coat.

"Now stick your hands in your armpits," Addison said buttoning Charlie's coat around him. "Shouldn't take long to warm you up. Then do like Jibway and Maybell. Keep your shooting hand warm and limber. Ride with it stuck inside your coat."

Addison guided Charlie's boot into the stirrup and hoisted him up. Then, he tied the reins of Charlie's horse to his saddle horn and set out after Maybell.

"You got us riding the spares," Charlie said, "Cause riding side-by-side we can't just follow the trail Jibway cut through the snow, cause our mounts gotta plow their own trail?"

Addison nodded, looked up, and checked the position of the sun.

Charlie again: "When we turn west, we want there to still be sun in the eyes of any shooter."

It hadn't been phrased as a question, but Addison nodded and turned his head to his left. He didn't want Charlie to see his smile. *Shoulda had Maybell beat up Orson. He'd have come around sooner.*

Jibway turned in the saddle and looked back. He pointed to his right. Addison couldn't see it but knew he pointed at the fence post demarking one-quarter mile north of Eighth Street, the point where the long-range-shooter patrol turned west.

Charlie squirmed a hand free, unbuttoned his coat, and put it on properly.

When they reached the fencepost, Addison had them dismount to switch horses again. He wanted Outlaw under him when they headed west. Still, no breeze sliced above the snow. Even a light breeze would have added brutality to the cold, but it would have enabled Outlaw to smell a shooter better.

Jibway and Maybell hadn't turned yet. Once they did, Addison and Charlie would mount and parallel them.

When Addison had discussed the morning's mission with his blood brother, they'd agreed that finding a shooter along the banks of the Delaware River was a possibility. It was far more likely to find one hiding opposite the Meeting House and/or opposite the new church on Eighth Street.

While they waited, Addison marched in the path plowed by Jibway's horse, giving his legs a little work to do. Charlie walked, too. When he'd gone far enough, Addison stopped intending to return to the horses.

Charlie stood in the middle of the trail. "I ain't never going back to the Last Chance Saloon."

During the drought last summer, Mr. Potts had added a *Last Chance Saloon* to his trading post. Reedley's son Maurice had said, "There's a Last Chance Saloon every hundred miles from here to Oregon." But the one some of the young Brotherton men had begun visiting was Potts'.

Charlie led the way back. "Preacher Cromwell said, 'Beer and whiskey are sleeping potions for a man's conscience.'"

Addison said, "Preacher Larrimer told us we have a problem in Brotherton. The problem is normalcy. When we first arrived here, there was so much work to do: building homes and the first church, setting up farms, and defending ourselves from the pro-slavers; there wasn't time to be normal. But now that we all have homes, and farms or businesses, we've settled into normalcy. And the devil uses normalcy as cover to sneak among us and sow the seeds of evil. I confess, Charlie, until he said that, I thought being normal was something to pray *for*."

Charlie walked around his horse. "Right now, I could use a cup of coffee. It would be a lot more than *normal* good."

Addison studied his … partner.

"Huh!" Charlie said. "You're lookin' at me like you're trying to figure out if I really changed or if I'm just acting like it. All I can say is, you go and get your nose busted by a girl. See if it don't change you, too."

Charlie looked past Addison. "Jibway and that girl turned. We best get moving. You want I should ride first?"

"Ride fifty yards back. Keep your eyes open. If you see something, holler, 'Duck!' Then you dive off your horse, too." Addison climbed up onto the saddle and started Outlaw. He stuck his gloved shooting hand into his coat pocket. To his right, Jibway and Maybell were stark black blobs on the sparkling snowscape. The other way, along Eighth Street, the snow-roofed houses and The Church of God Most Holy laid down a sharp boundary between Brotherton and the uncivilized prairie. He could also see his tiny house at the end of Main Street, where Mariah and Hope waited.

Addison J. Freeman! He faced west, not wanting Charlie to tell him to pay attention to the work at hand.

In the distance, about even with the new church, and just to the left of Outlaw's ear, a flash of reflected sunlight stabbed his eyes. Addison dove off to his right. Before he hit the ground, he heard, "Duck!" Then his face smacked into the snow. His shooting hand had gotten stuck in the coat pocket and had been unable to prevent him landing face-first.

The snow cushioned the blow from the ground. "Outlaw. Down." He freed his hand, grabbed the reins, and pulled, and the horse settled onto his knees and rolled onto his side.

A sharp crack blasted across the snow. Behind him, Charlie's horse screamed.

"You all right, Charlie?"

"Yeah. Horse ain't, though."

Looking ahead, Addison saw a tendril of smoke rising straight up as if creating a pointer. He unslung his rifle, checked to see that the barrel hadn't been jammed full of snow, checked that he had a round chambered, pulled the glove off his shooting hand, jumped to his feet, aimed at the base of the gun smoke pointer, fired, and dropped down again. Charlie fired also. Then Jibway fired, or maybe it had been Maybell. Another shot sounded from the direction of town. The rifleman in the bell tower of the church.

Addison waited in the snow hole he'd created. He hoped the pro-slavery shooter would fire again. The man's gun was a single shot. He was pretty sure. Firing while the man was reloading, that's what he wanted to do.

A shot rang out. From the north. Jibway. Charlie fired again, and so did Church Tower Shooter.

Outlaw was trying to get his legs under him. "Stay down!"

Another shot fired. From the north again. Addison peeked above the snow. The gun smoke pointer had returned. Charlie fired. Church Tower Shooter fired. *What are you waiting for Addison?* He got a knee under him, aimed, and fired. Then, he stood and fired until he was empty. Just before he dropped to the ground, he caught a glimpse of Jibway on his big black, hunched low across the animal's back and firing a pistol.

Addison lay on his back and reloaded. Then he rolled through the snow, away from Outlaw, and rose to a knee.

Jibway sat upright in the saddle, aiming a pistol at a man standing in front of him. Maybell rode toward her husband. Behind him, Charlie was running toward Jibway. Behind Charlie, both his and Addison's spare horses galloped back toward the river.

"Up!" Addison said, and Outlaw got clumsily but rapidly to his feet, and shivered mightily, shaking snow from his chest and belly.

Charlie was almost up to him. He held his rifle in his hand and was sort of loping through the deep snow.

"Stop, Charlie!"

Charlie—he almost thought of him as the McTavish kid, but he wasn't a kid anymore. *Another but: he still has a coupla' things to learn.* Addison slung his rifle across his back, mounted from the right side, and rode to next to Charlie.

McTavish leaned on his butt down rifle huffing out rapid, regular white puffs like a locomotive climbing a hill. Addison removed his foot from the stirrup, extended a hand, pulled the man up to behind him, and started Outlaw toward Jibway, Maybell, and a man standing with his hands raised.

As they approached, about ten yards closer to town than Hands Raised, Addison saw a man lying on his back. He had a bullet hole in his forehead and a long gun next to him. It looked as if he'd been lying on a buffalo robe and had had another over him with snow on top of it.

Mr. Hands Raised looked to be about thirty. He wore a bushy black beard and a white scarf across the top of his head and knotted under his chin. Buttons from the man's coat flew as Maybell ripped it open. She removed his belt gun from its holster, stuck it in a pocket of her own coat, knelt, and pulled a knife from the man's boot.

As Maybell rose to her feet, Jibway said, "What's your name?"

Hands Raised had scared black eyes. They darted about as if looking for the answer to the question.

Maybell ripped off the man's scarf and said, "Name. Or I'll cut off an ear."

The fear departed the black eyes. Clearly, he felt he had nothing to be afraid of from this snippet of a black girl blustering empty threats. As sudden as the strike of a rattlesnake that had its rattles pulled off, Maybell grabbed his ear and slashed with the knife.

"Ow! Oh!"

She hadn't cut it all the way off, but the wound bled. Copiously.

"Name," Maybell demanded.

He lowered one hand. The other cupped his bleeding ear.

The fear had returned to the man's eyes, Addison noted, along with cunning.

"Axelrod. Amos Axelrod."

"Prevaricator!" Maybell said and shot her right fist at the man's nose.

The man yowled and fell back onto the snow.

"I almost feel sorry him," Charlie said.

Addison said, "Jibway, Maybell, Charlie's sweating. I'm going to take him to the sheriff's office before he freezes to death."

As Outlaw started plowing through the snow, Addison heard, "Myron Walsh. I'm Myron Walsh."

*****

"What happened to you?" Marshal McTavish asked his son.

"Fell asleep. Fell out of the saddle and landed on my face," Charlie replied.

"Marshal," Addison cut in, "he was sweating and shivering something fierce when we rode up. We need to get him warmed up."

The marshal shook his head. "You fell out of your saddle and broke your nose and then you started sweating! What in blue blazes is going on here?"

"Marshal," Addison pushed himself back into the conversation, "We killed a long-range shooter. Jibway and Maybell are questioning his spotter. The spotter's name is Myron Walsh. I need to find Joshua Reedley and see if Mr. Walsh is on the paroled list."

"Go find Joshua," the marshal said. "I'll take care of my boy."

Addison thought but didn't say: *He ain't no boy no more.* He opened the door and quickly closed it behind him. *Maybe Maybell will teach me how to speak properly. Ma will be pleased if she does.*

He rode Outlaw to the Meeting House. Reedley was not there, but Addison deployed one of the Safety Committee men to find him and ask Joshua to come to Marshal McTavish's office. Then he remounted Outlaw and headed north back down C Street. When he crossed Third Street, he saw a mounted stranger holding the reins to another horse at the corner of Third and B Streets, near the steps leading into church. He turned and rode toward the man. The man didn't look at him as he approached.

Addison ripped his glove off and drew his belt gun from inside his coat. He stopped Outlaw. "Who are you, mister, and what are you doing here?"

The man turned but didn't answer. Addison gigged Outlaw with his heels, crowded alongside, grabbed the man, and jerked him off his horse. Dismounting, he pushed the stranger ahead of him up the steps, and said, "Open the door."

He opened it. Another stranger had one hand on the door from the vestibule to inside the church and a pistol in the other. He raised his gun. Addison raised his. The man beside him grabbed his gun hand, forcing it down.

Addison stepped behind the man he'd unhorsed. Inside Stranger fired and the bullet struck his partner. Addison freed his gun hand, fired, and the gunman fell to the floor.

Hand Grabber lay on his back. He moaned. Inside Gunman was on his side, not moving.

Addison ripped open the moaner's coat, took his belt gun, did a quick check for other weapons, found none, and took the steps up and into the vestibule in a single stride.

The would-be shooter had his back against the door into the church, a pistol in his left hand. Addison laid the gun aside. The man's dull, dead eyes had frozen in a blind man's stare. A moment ago, hate had probably burned bright in those windows to the man's soul, but nothing burned there now.

From inside the church, someone tried to push open the door, but the body blocked it.

"Just a minute!" Addison shouted, grabbed the dead man's legs, and dragged him out of the way.

The door flew open, and Mayor Argyl glanced at Addison, then at the man on the floor. "What—"

The sound of a horse pounding hard down C Street cut off the mayor.

Addison hurried to the outside door, shifted his pistol to his left hand, and peered around the jamb.

A horse squatted on its haunches, skidding on the snow. Maybell

Jim hopped from the saddle, pistol in her hand, and stepped onto the boardwalk in front of the church. She stopped when she saw Addison.

"Did they kill Preacher Larrimer?" she said.

Preacher Larrimer answered the question. "No." He descended the steps. Mariah and a crowd followed him.

Mariah knelt by the man lying on the outside top step, pulled the scarf from around her neck, and pressed it over the stomach wound. "He's bleeding inside. I can't stop that."

"Maybell," Mayor Argyl said, "what spurred you here in such a hurry?"

They'd come across a long-range shooter and his spotter, she reported in a stampede of words. They were going to kill Preacher Cromwell. Another two bushwhackers were going to shoot Preacher Larrimer.

"The marshal sent me to warn you." Maybell nodded to the preacher and sucked in a big breath.

The crowd buzzed like a bumped hive.

Larrimer directed his congregation to return to their pews and two men to carry the wounded man inside the church. They placed him on the floor at the front by the penance pew. The preacher knelt beside him. "My son, if you are truly sorry for your sins, God will forgive you."

The man opened his eyes. Short, shallow breaths huffed in and out of his open mouth.

Larrimer said, "God has given you time to save your soul. Do not let this opportunity pass you by."

"We wuz gonna git a hunnerd dollars each fer shootin' you."

Addison wanted to shout, "From who?" But he kept his mouth shut.

The dying man raised a hand and grasped the preacher's arm. "Forgive me?"

The preacher said, "I forgive you, but you must ask the Lord to forgive you."

The man's hand dropped from Larrimer's arm. Palpable, solemn silence filled New Found Grace Church. Mariah knelt beside the man opposite the preacher and checked. Then she shook her head.

In the third pew from the front, the Tanber boy, he was eleven, Addison thought, asked his mother, "Do you think he's in heaven?"

Larrimer said, "God our father, Lord of heaven and earth, please accept the soul of this repentant sinner." He stood and faced the congregation. "When we get to heaven, we will all know the answer to young Mr. Tanber's question."

Preacher Larrimer then took his place behind the podium.

At the same moment, Addison realized he'd brought guns into the church. Maybell did, too. They returned to the vestibule and hung their gun belts on hooks.

When they came back inside, Larrimer was entreating the Lord to help the country fill the gulf of hatred, dividing the people into what were clearly two separate nations. "Help us to know, Lord, peace in our time."

24

Addison and Maybell walked their horses side-by-side, heading down C Street. Addison had nothing to say. Neither, apparently, did Maybell.

As they looped reins over the hitching post outside, Preacher Cromwell stepped out of the marshal's office. "Preacher Larrimer?"

"He's all right," Addison answered.

"Thanks to him." Maybell hooked a thumb.

Cromwell bowed his head and whispered, "Thank You most gracious Lord." He raised his head and smiled a little. "God bless you, Mr. Freeman." Then, he crossed the street to the church.

Inside the marshal's office, Addison found Charlie seated and his father standing next to him. The marshal glanced at them as Maybell closed the door. McTavish handed his son a pair of socks.

Addison pulled off his gloves and unbuttoned his coat but didn't take it off. "Jibway?"

"Hasn't come in yet," Charlie snugged up the second sock.

"Preacher Larrimer?" the marshal said.

"The preacher's fine," Maybell replied, "Two men did try to shoot him, but Addison shot them first."

McTavish: "The two men?"

Maybell: "Dead."

"Did you get their names?"

"No."

An annoyed look decorated the marshal's face.

Addison: "One of the bushwhackers died outright. The other one lingered a bit, but Preacher Larrimer wanted to save his soul."

"And you thought that was more important than finding out who these assassins were and who sent them?"

The deputy marshal and the marshal locked eyes. McTavish looked away first. Addison started buttoning his coat. "I'm gonna check on Jibway."

Maybell opened the door and stepped out with Addison right behind her.

"Wait," Charlie said. "I'll go with you."

"Catch up." Addison closed the door.

Outlaw walked in the trail plowed through the snow previously. As they crossed Eighth Street, Addison turned in the saddle, removed his hand from inside his coat, and waved to the bell tower lookout. He waved back.

When they arrived at the spot where the long-range shooter and his spotter had hidden, Addison moved Outlaw to the side and studied the signs in the packed, blood-stained snow.

The shooter no longer lay atop his buffalo hide. The hide was spotted with blood stains. Three splotches. One on the left, one on the right, and the other where the head would have been. *The head wound, one of my ... or one of Charlie's rounds.* Addison grudgingly surrendered to the possibility.

The bell tower lookout put a bullet into the man. The other wound would have been from Jibway. Or Maybell. He looked at her. She stared back. *Maybell then.*

The spotter had hidden a couple of yards beyond the shooter, creating a second area of disturbed snow. There was no blood on the buffalo hides there, but at the edge of the packed snow, a large red stain had been melted and frozen into the snow.

Beyond where the two bushwhackers had hidden, horses had cut two trails to the spot. One of those trails had sign of something like logs being dragged back north. Both log trails had been stained with bright red blood.

As far as Addison knew, the spotter had not been wounded. He studied the signs in the snow and considered possible causes for what he saw.

Maybell said, "Jibway asked the spotter questions."

Addison said, "He needed persuasion to answer."

And the man had not survived the persuasion. The log trails were made by bodies, not tree trunks. Addison did not think it necessary to voice those thoughts. Neither did Maybell.

To the north, in the distance, he spied a black blob, stark against the everywhere white. Addison pulled his binoculars from the saddlebag. He couldn't make out the rider but recognized Jibway's horse. Two other horses trailed behind the big black. He lowered the glasses intending to offer them to Maybell, but she kicked her mount with her heels, and it sprang into a gallop down the trail between the two log-drag troughs. He followed her.

*****

Addison, Jibway, and Maybell stomped snow off their boots and entered the marshal's office. Besides McTavish father and son, Joshua Reedley waited there as well. The marshal sat behind his desk. Reedley sat on one of six chairs at a round table. As the newcomers shucked coats, hats, scarves, and gloves, Charlie poured coffee into tin cups on the table.

Jibway pulled a chair back, sat, and sipped. "Ah! White man coffee!"

Addison looked at Reedley. Joshua's expression remained passive, but Addison knew he also read the Indian's words not as gratitude for the blessed brew but as a comment that, *After everything the white man brought us, disease, greed, and hatred, finally something good and useful: coffee.*

After Addison and Maybell took seats, Jibway related how, after the long-range shooter killed Charlie's horse, he and Maybell rode toward the church. The long-range shooter had been struck three times. Once by the bell tower lookout, once by Maybell, and once by either Addison or Charlie.

"Charlie," Addison said.

Jibway continued. The shooter's spotter was Myron Walsh. He confessed that they had been sent to kill the two preachers in Brotherton. Maybell had ridden to warn Preacher Larrimer.

Maybell cut in and reported what Addison had done.

Jibway resumed his narrative. After Maybell departed, he continued to question Walsh. His partner's name was Tilman Wiggins, and they were to kill Preacher Cromwell. They'd been paid twenty-five dollars and would get another hundred if they succeeded. Willie Newsome and George Stallworth aimed to assassinate Preacher Larrimer.

"Myron Walsh disclosed one other bit of information," Jibway reported. "A man named Walter Standish had been wounded in a shootout with John Brown near Topeka some years back. Walter was paralyzed from the waist down. Had to wear a diaper ever since. He hated abolitionists and would spend all his fortune to wipe out Brotherton. If the preachers were eliminated, he figured the people of Brotherton would be dispirited and go back east where they came from. If they wouldn't go, he'd keep trying to exterminate them."

Marshal McTavish exclaimed a string of harsh-sounding foreign words. He'd once confessed from the penance pew that he swore, on occasion, but when he did so, it was in Gaelic. So the youngsters wouldn't learn blasphemous words.

Addison recalled Deacon Agatha Janson's reply: "Best to not swear at all."

As if she'd read his mind, Maybell said. "Damnation! Sometimes won't nothing do for a person but a good *Damnation!*"

"Walter Standish!" Marshal McTavish snarled.

Addison had never noted before that a man could cuss with his eyes.

*****

In their bedroom, Addison held Mariah as she sobbed.

In their other bedroom, Hope wailed. Awakened by her mother's crying. He felt as if his heart had two fishhooks in it pulling in opposite directions. Just then, though, he needed to stay with the baby's mother.

"This feels much worse than all the other things you've done." She wiped her nose on the sleeve of her nightgown.

"We're just going to Atchison to scout for a Hostetler wagon train. Like I've done—"

"Liar! Maybell told me the truth. Why don't you?"

Hope's calls for attention had not caused the timely response she expected, so she raised the level of her protest.

"I'm going to get the baby. Then, I will. I'll tell you the truth."

As Addison changed the inconsolable infant, she fussed herself red-faced. When she finally stopped crying to nurse, the ensuing silence was something he could hear.

The silence sounded sort of like, but different than, the nighttime buzz and hum of summer insects. He was anxious to share this discovery with Mariah. She'd want to hear about it. Well, after he explained his prevarication.

He sighed and waited while she fed the child, burped her, and returned her to her cradle.

Why did Maybell tell her they were going after Walter Standish?

Only McTavish father and son, Joshua Reedley, Jibway and Maybell, and Addison had been in the marshal's office when Jibway related what he'd learned from the spotter, Myron Walsh. There was no legal authority in the Kansas Territory they could take the information to and expect any kind of justice to result. Reedley decided a small party had to go after Walter Standish. He would only take those in the room with him. The marshal, of course, would not go, but everyone in the room swore not to disclose the mission to anyone else. Not even to a best friend, a parent, or a spouse. They were going to take the law, such as it was, into their own hands, and the fewer people aware of that the better for all of them.

So why had Maybell broken her oath?

It was quiet in the other bedroom. Hope's little world had been set right again. Now it was time to see if he could set his big world with his wife right again. He sighed—It was a night for sighing—and went to the kitchen and sat at the table.

Mariah brought the lamp and placed it between them. She held up the thumb of her left hand. A fresh cut mark stood out red down the middle.

He frowned. "You and Maybell—"

"Are blood sisters."

"And that—"

"Bond is more sacred than an oath made to men."

Addison rose, took a butcher knife from a drawer, and returned. He slashed a bleeding cross bar over the old scar in the meat of his left thumb. Then, he took Mariah's hand and looked at her. She stared right back. He interpreted it as assent and sliced a cross bar onto the vertical line already there and pressed the thumbs together.

He looked into her eyes. "I will never lie to you again." And he told her about Standish.

She bandaged his thumb with a strip of cloth. He bandaged hers. They went to bed then. At three a.m., he rose, kissed her, dressed, and left the house to saddle Outlaw.

Fifteen minutes later, Reedley, Jibway and Maybell, and Charlie McTavish rode down Main Street, each of them leading a spare horse. Except Charlie led two, one of them for Addison.

The two days since the attempted preacher assassinations had been warm. A good bit of the snow had melted. However, at night, the temperature dipped below freezing. The road to the ferry crossing consisted of ice-crusted mud. Hooves busted through the crust. Thankfully, the footing wasn't treacherous. All the horses, though, wore Joshua Reedley leather horse boots.

The ferry across the Delaware River waited on the west bank for them.

Once across, Reedley pushed them through the day and into the night. They ate and rested for three hours and rose again to arrive in Atchison at midmorning.

They sought out Ziggy Hostetler first. Reedley explained their purpose. Ziggy left the men resting and went to confer with Norb Bass, the man in charge of the wagon train staging lot.

Ziggy returned at noon accompanied by Bart Finch. Finch would lead the Brotherton posse to the man they sought.

The group crossed the Missouri and headed south the rest of the day and through the night. Two additional nights of moonlit, slow, and careful travel brought them to Standish's Mansion before sunrise.

Their guide had brought them to the edge of a forest about two hundred yards from the Standish place.

The front of the tall, two-story house was to the left. Moonlight gilded gray over the white pillars supporting a roof over a broad porch spanning the width of the building. The siding was also gilded-gray white. Large, dark windows looked out of the bottom and top floors of the front. There were no windows on the side they faced.

A large barn, as tall as the house, sat behind the mansion. A row of small structures lined the near side of the barn. Another row of shacks lined the far side.

"Slave quarters?" Charlie whispered.

Addison nodded.

"I'll scout one side," Reedley whispered to Jibway. "Which side you want?"

Jibway unslung his rifle and bow from across his back, strung the bow, stuck the long gun in the scabbard tied to his saddle, handed the reins of his big black to Maybell, and headed toward the barn.

Reedley walked bent over toward the road leading up to the front of the Standish house.

"He's walking that way," Charlie whispered, "in case somebody sees him? They'd think his shadow was maybe an animal, right? If he stood upright, wouldn't be any question he was a man."

Addison clamped a hand over Charlie's blabber mouth and held it there for a moment before taking it a way.

"Sorry."

Addison turned his back to Charlie. In a situation like this, you maintained silence. Questions should be saved till later. *Don't make noise.* If you had to speak, you kept it short. *And keep your mind totally on the task at hand.* That was the other important thing, and he, Addison J. Freeman, seasoned scout, had allowed the McTavish kid to distract him.

Reedley crossed the road and disappeared into the forest. In the other direction, he couldn't see Jibway, either. Both of them could be gone for a while.

Maybell watched the mansion and scanned to her left and right. Doing, Addison knew, what Jibway had taught her. Using all her senses, including one or two she didn't even know she possessed. Her spirit would be feeling for the spirit of an approaching enemy. She'd have turned off her eyes, ears, and sense of smell. For a moment. Addison watched her until she moved her head. That meant she'd reactivated her eyes and other physical senses.

Addison then led Charlie to where Bart Finch waited with the horses. Enough moonlight filtered through the bare limbs of the overhead trees for hand signals. Bart and Charlie were to grab some shuteye. One hour.

Bart untied the roll behind his saddle, draped the cloth over his shoulders, and sat with his back against a tree. Charlie did the same. Without talking.

Addison went to Maybell and signed for her to get some sleep. She wrapped her bedroll around her and leaned against a tree quicker than a scared squirrel could climb it. Then he probed the darkness for enemies and for Joshua and Jibway.

An hour passed. A swath of red smeared the eastern sky. He was about to wake Maybell when he sensed something off to his right. The back of his neck felt like bugs were crawling through his hair. Addison was sure something was out there. An animal? A raccoon, maybe. Or a man. He drew his pistol but didn't cock it. Because of the noise it would make.

About thirty yards away, the figure of a man rose above the waist-high brush. Addison cocked his weapon. The man shadow raised something above his head. A long gun. Or a bow. *Jibway!*

"Come," Addison said just loud enough to cover the distance.

Maybell rolled out of her blankets and stood with her rifle in her hands.

Jibway lowered his hand, hunkered over, and moved toward his blood brother.

Addison's blood brother wanted a powwow with the others. After he woke the two sleepers, Jibway reported what he'd learned. "They have no sentries out, and I counted thirty shacks, slave quarters. Only four of those were occupied."

"Word is, "Bart said, "Standish wanted to sell the place along with the slaves, but nobody could roust up enough money. So, he sold off most of the slaves. Kept a handful to manage the garden, chickens, and such. Plus, he's got a couple of house_" Bart Finch paused and glanced at Maybell. "Negroes," he finished off his sentence.

"Anybody else inside the house?" Jibway said.

"Word is he employs some white guys. A handful, maybe."

It was light enough to see Jibway's expression as he rubbed his chin, in the white man's way when thinking.

"I'm taking Maybell with me to talk to the people in the shacks." He looked at his blood brother. "You stay here."

That last was a question, a suggestion, and an order all rolled into one.

Jibway and Maybell moved away through the brush. She made a little noise. *About what I'd make.*

Addison stared at the mansion. Still, nothing stirred around it. No sign of Reedley. From the far side, a rooster crowed *wake up* to the world. He, however, took a nap.

Wrapped in his bedroll, leaning against a tree, he left his pistols in their holsters. If he woke suddenly, he would know where the guns were and not have to grope for them in the bedding. Exhaustion sought to claim him, to pull him deep, but he resisted. Even if Jibway or Maybell were on watch, he would not allow himself to sink deep. He did think, *Good night, Mariah. Good night, Hope.* Then, he rudely shoved them to the back of his mind against the skull.

It seemed but an instant later when a sudden rattle jerked him alert.

Addison threw off his bedroll, jumped up, and drew a pistol and cocked it. Charlie and Bart stared at a wagon rumbling down the dirt road leading from the mansion. A broad-shouldered, giant white man held the reins to the team. He looked big enough to pull the wagon himself. As the wagon passed by with a jangle of trace chains, Addison lowered the hammer on his gun.

"Going for supplies," Charlie whisper-mused.

At least he's thinking the right things. Now, if I can just get him to do keep-your-darned-mouth-shut thinking!

Addison sensed someone behind him. He spun around, dropped to a knee, and re-cocked his pistol.

Reedley stood beside a tree with his hands raised.

A few minutes later, Jibway and Maybell returned accompanied by a young colored woman named Becca.

Reedley huddled everyone up a few steps toward where the horses were tethered. Maybell carried a flour sack. Addison smelled bacon. His mouth watered. Becca carried a jug of coffee. She also carried a flour sack with tin cups wrapped in cloth.

"Miss Becca," Joshua whispered. "Serve these two first, please." He pointed to Jibway and Addison.

Then, Reedley posted Jibway at the edge of the trees facing the mansion.

Addison occupied a lookout spot just beyond the horses. After nothing but cold camps since they left Atchison, the coffee was … well, it was the second-best thing in the world. First best would have been coffee with Mariah and Hope in his kitchen. *Lookout Freeman, look out.* He sipped. Then, he looked out.

Becca's subdued voice reached Addison.

Besides herself, eight other Colored people lived in the shacks on the far side of the barn. Two of them were her mammy and pappy. All of them were old, too old to fetch a good price when Massa Standish sold off the others. Inside the house, Massa kept two more Coloreds plus four white men. All the white men did was serve as guards. The Coloreds took care of Massa and the house and cooked. Massa had a room on the ground floor. The whites had second-story bedrooms. The Coloreds had rooms in the cellar. Then, Reedley asked questions.

"The white men. They ever have to fight off outlaws, thieves, that sort?"

"No, *suh*. Onliest thing I ever seed them do is run off beggars."

"The wagon that left earlier. He going for supplies?"

"Yes, sir. Wagon goes once a week."

"What about visitors? Do people come to see Mr. Standish?"

"No, suh. After Massa got his-self crippled up, they stopped coming."

Reedley called Addison and Jibway to join the group and explained his plan.

*****

The supply wagon always returned just before dark. Reedley's plan called for action to commence during dinner time. The meal started promptly at noon, and a half hour later, the Massa and his guest guard would be drinking coffee and brandy and smoking a cigar. Joshua assigned Jibway to a lookout post on the opposite side of the mansion. Bart Finch watched up the road the wagon had followed.

The people in the shacks knew Reedley's plan. The inside-the-house servants didn't.

Maybell, dressed in one of Becca's dresses and carrying a basket of eggs, would enter the rear door into the mansion at light-the-cigars time. Addison would creep up to the house on the windowless side, crawl under the windows in the rear, and position himself to follow Maybell inside. Addison would subdue the dinner-guest guard, hopefully without making noise. Then, he and Maybell would take on the upstairs guards. That was the plan.

At the rear door, Addison rose to his feet, pulled a pistol, cocked it, and nodded to Maybell. In the kitchen, a Colored woman—Amber—washed dishes at a counter. She turned with a smile blooming across her face. Then, her eyes lit on Addison.

Maybell said, "We're not going to hurt you, Amber."

Joshua had said Maybell being Colored and using Amber's name would be enough to keep the woman from screaming.

Reedley was right. *He is most of the time.*

The door from the dining room pushed open. A Negro man, well dressed, with white hair, stood still as his eyes darted about the room. He frowned at Maybell. Then he saw Addison and dropped the stack of dirty plates he carried.

"What the hell, Ambrose!" blasted from the dining room. "Give him a caning, Will. Maybe it'll learn him to be more careful."

Ambrose. Becca had explained that Massa had a way of naming his Coloreds. The house servants had names beginning with "A." She and her parents had "B" names and lived in the first of the row of shacks alongside the barn. "C" names lived in the next house.

That thought had flitted through Addison's brain as he hurried to grab Ambrose, pull him into the kitchen, and close the door.

As boots clomped across the dining room floor, Addison lowered the hammer on his gun.

The door swung open. Addison smashed the butt of his pistol on the man's nose. He howled and fell back. Maybell jumped over the fallen man, ran to Standish seated at the head of the table, and wrenched a derringer from his hand.

The guy on the floor, Will, rolled onto his side, hiked up his pant leg, and reached for the handle of a gun in his boot.

Addison dropped his pistol, drew his belt knife, grabbed a handful of Will's hair, jerked his head back, and cut his throat. He did not want to alert the upstairs guards just yet.

Standish hollered, "Get your goddamned—" and his mouth spewed spittle and vile and vicious words, and his eyes blazed hate at Maybell. Until she cocked the derringer, stuck it in the slave owner's mouth, and pulled the trigger.

Addison followed the sound of the upstairs guards running. One man, pistol drawn and pointing, appeared at the top of the stairs. Addison shot him. A second man reached a pistol under the ceiling and fired two rounds, then he descended hunkered over and fired a blind round with each step lower. Addison shot him in the leg. This man howled and tumbled down the rest of the steps. Addison hoped they could take this man alive. Reedley had questions.

Addison hurried to his last target and checked him. Dead. Broken neck by the look of him. The wagon driver, Reedley would have to get his answers from him.

Joshua's new plan called for him and Jibway to intercept the wagon and persuade the driver to give up the information they needed: What other people were involved in funding, organizing, and deploying gangs of pro-slavers to attack Brotherton?

While they were occupied with that task, Addison and the rest of the Brotherton posse would get help from Standish's just-emancipated slaves and bury the plantation guards in a well-hidden spot. Next, Bart Finch would draft up a Bill of Sale, with a forged signature, transferring ownership of the eleven slaves to Reedley. According to Joshua, all the slaves were now free, but papers documenting their status would not be written until they returned to Brotherton.

Once the burying was finished, Addison was to search for additional wagons and ready up to four of them for the return to Brotherton.

The shed behind the barn contained a number of wagons. The barn, however, contained only two teams of draft animals, along with the mounts for the guards. Plus, they had their own spare horses. Addison sent Charlie to select two pairs from the riding stock, which seemed most likely to accept harnessing. At the same time, he had the men from the B to E houses hoist up the four in-best-shape wagons and greasing the axels. The four men were all gray-haired, but they worked like twenty-year-olds who were promised bonuses if they finished their jobs in a hurry.

By the time Reedley and Jibway drove the supply wagon to the front of the mansion, without the driver, Addison had four wagons hitched to teams. The wagons were loaded with food, clothing, and bedding.

"No furniture," Addison had said when asked. "We want to keep the loads light."

Reedley checked the wagons, nodded his approval, and said, "Time to get moving."

Addison was to scout ahead, Maybell to guard the rear. Becca wanted to ride with her. Maybell nodded her approval.

With sun sliding below the edge of the world, they set off, heading north with Bart Finch driving the supply wagon. The other wagons trailed with those not driving or scouting, sleeping. The horses, too, took turns in harness. The extra saddle mounts seemed to prefer the harness to being dragged along by a rope around their necks.

Just after sunrise, they stopped, lit fires, and fixed breakfast and coffee. The wagon train started rolling again two hours later, but headed northwest now instead of due north. Reedley's plan was to skirt the heavily populated area around Kansas City and head directly for Brotherton. Joshua left Addison in charge of the wagons. Reedley and Jibway rode ahead toward Leavenworth. There, they intended to meet up with a man named Vern Chapman. He was, they had learned, Standish's agent who deployed pro-slavery gangs against Brotherton.

Addison had Bart Finch scout ahead of the train. Charlie guarded the rear. Becca drove the supply wagon. Maybell rode next to the last wagon. Her pistol was hidden in the folds of her dress, and her long gun was stashed under the driver's bench. She'd help Charlie if needed. Addison would aid Finch if he required assistance.

That afternoon, Finch rode beside Addison and reported, "Up ahead, fellow named Abercrombie has a scratch-dirt farm. He almost shot me. Thought I was a Red Leg, Abolitionist, or a Free Stater. Jayhawkers stole his horses and most everything he had to eat. So, he's got a barn with a loft still half full of hay. I told him we would give him four horses and some vittles if we could overnight our animals in his barn."

Addison nodded. "The horses could stand a night to recover. And we're far enough away from the Standish place. We can spare the horses. You think we'll be safe there?"

"Yep. We're still a ways from any settled area. But us white guys need to act like slave owners, and our Colored folks need to act like slaves. I'm worried about Maybell."

"I'll talk to her. And Abercrombie. He by himself?"

"No. A wife. She can't have kids he told me. When he said that, she hung her head. I got the notion Abercrombie treats his wife worse than Standish treated his slaves." Finch shook his head. "Prairie farming's hard on a woman. Not another female to talk to and a woman's work, like the saying goes, is never done. I've seen more than a few shriveled, dried-up women like her. Always makes me think of the fig tree Jesus cursed."

The words *shriveled and dried-up* started a parade of thoughts in Addison's head. Mariah, Ma, Hope, Lizbeth. The first three he said a quick prayer for the Lord to save them from such a fate. For Lizbeth, he couldn't keep the notion that his pa and hers had shriveled Lizbeth and killed her even more effectively than the prairie could have.

"What're you thinking, Addison? You wanna stop at Abercrobie's?"

"Yes. The horses, all of us could use a good night's rest."

*****

Two days later, Reedley and Jibway caught up to the wagon train at mid-morning, two hours short of reaching the ferry crossing of the Delaware near Brotherton.

Addison said," Mr. Reedley," and "How."

Joshua nodded. His blood brother rolled his eyes.

"Any trouble along the way?" Reedley said.

"No," the wagon master replied. "A sheriff did ask to see our bills of sale for the Colored people once, but he didn't try to detain us."

Addison didn't ask them about Leavenworth. The entire wagon train knew what had happened at the Standish place. That couldn't be helped, but there was no need for anyone else to know what Reedley and Jibway had done. Joshua, however, offered, "It was taken care of."

After they crossed the river, the last wagons were guided to the Meeting House to join the earlier arrivals in a celebratory meal. Following supper, Preacher Larrimer conducted an evening service of thanksgiving for the arrival of new citizens of Brotherton. Then, the Meeting House needed to be cleaned, and Mariah and Addison pitched in with that chore.

And finally, they were able to go home. It didn't take long to get Hope down. Then Addison and Mariah went to bed.

"Are you mad at me for being gone so long?"

"I was going to be."

*****

Reedley insisted Brotherton maintain a state of high vigilance for a month; then, with no sign of long-range shooters or of large pro-slavery gangs, he agreed to a relaxation of the patrols to a more normal state of watchfulness. As soon as that happened, Addison and Mariah went to Preacher Larrimer and requested a church service thanking the Lord for bringing them safely to Kansas, protecting them during repeated assaults by the pro-slavers, and entreating Him to give them a period of peace.

Mariah wanted a special prayer added. A plea to the Almighty that the people of Brotherton would never again have to serve as parole breaker executioners.

Preacher Larrimer agreed that such a service was not only appropriate but needed. He invited Preacher Cromwell to co-minister. Cromwell bowed his head, accepting.

The service was conducted outdoors so that everyone could attend. The preachers spoke from a platform built by Otto Vogelsang.

That night at supper, with Hope in her basket on the table, Mariah said, "During the service, I felt cleansed, forgiven."

"Normal?" Addison suggested.

"Better than normal. I feel right with God."

Addison took her hand and kissed it. He was happy for her. For himself, though, it wasn't for him to say he was right with God. He did sense a pre-crusade normalcy. An all-the-way-back-to-Illinois normalcy. Before the killing began. And that was good enough for him.

1861

Insistent, persistent church bell clanging woke Addison and Mariah. And Hope.

"Please, God. Not again."

Addison knew what Mariah prayed for: that the bells did not signal an attack by the Kansas pro-slavery faction. February the sixth. For almost a whole year, Brotherton had known peace. For a whole year, almost, neither of them had had to kill a man. He threw the covers back, pulled on trousers and boots without taking the time for socks.

Mariah got out of bed to tend to their distraught daughter.

The bell kept up a steady ringing. If it was warning of an attack, the steady ringing should have stopped, and separate one, two, three, or four peals would have told of the direction from which the attack was coming. But the frantic dinging and donging continued. He pulled his coat on over his undershirt, said goodbye to Mariah as she changed their still screaming little stinker. He grabbed his hat from the peg by the door, and almost forgot to take his belt gun.

He stepped outside and closed the door. It was pitch-black dark out. After the lamplit living room, it took a moment for his eyes to adjust. Strapping on his belt gun, the thought of running to the church occurred, but he hustled to the horse shed, and mounted Outlaw bareback and galloped down Second Street to the church.

There he found a string of supply wagons lined up on C Street, and Ziggy Hostetler standing by Preacher Larrimer on the church steps.

A crowd of mostly dressed men streamed toward the church from all directions. Outlaw was the only horse attending.

"Congress voted eight days ago," Larrimer boomed. "Kansas has entered the Union as a free state! Praise be to God Almighty!"

It took a second for the news to register. Then, Addison noted the flow of men stop moving toward the church. He felt an urge to tell Mariah right away. By that time, though, a crowd had pressed in around him. He slipped off the horse's back and started pushing through packed men.

"Outlaw, try not to step on anyone." He'd said it loud.

Men moved out of the way, and Addison started running. After a few steps, he knew he was growing blisters on his heels, but that did not matter. Telling Mariah the news, that mattered.

*****

Preachers Larrimer and Cromwell held services of thanksgiving in their respective churches at ten a.m. Addison and Mariah Freeman attended New Found Grace. Jibway and Maybell Jim attended The Church of God Most Holy.

After the services, a communal dinner was served in the Meeting House. Following that, Ziggy Hostetler and his crew departed for Atchison, and Mariah invited Jibway and Maybell for coffee.

Once they were all seated at the Freeman's table, Jibway asked if he could hold Hope.

Addison glanced at Mariah. She twisted her head a half-turn. He thought it was going to be a "no" gesture. He said, "She's a fussy child."

But Mariah handed over the baby.

Sometimes Jibway wore his hair white man short. He currently wore his hair in braids dangling over the front of his shoulders. Just like Maybell had hers.

Hope seemed fascinated by the braids, and as Jibway took her, she took one of the braids in her little hand. Jibway let Hope pull on the braid, but he did stop her from putting it in her mouth.

Mariah sliced up coffee cake and put a plate in front of the adults. She poured "white man" coffee for Jibway and the others. Then she sat and took a sip of her coffee.

Maybell said, "We're pregnant."

Mariah started coughing. Addison jumped up to pat her on the back.

"Sorry," she said. "I … I was just surprised."

Maybell's and Jibway's eyes adored each other.

Addison grinned big. "Congratulations to you both." Pause. "Blood Brother, you are a man of many talents."

"I happy to be redskin. You no see me blush."

Hope tried again for a taste of hair, but Jibway stopped her again. Addison thought his daughter was about to express her frustrated desire.

"I'm pregnant, too," Mariah said.

Addison's forkful of coffee cake stopped its ascent and the utensil clattered onto his plate.

"I was going to tell you tonight. But, well—"

While the blood sisters gabbled unmitigated and shared joy and congratulation, the blood brothers' eyes met.

They were both thinking the same thing. Heaped atop a full year, almost, of peaceful existence in Brotherton, two new babies were too much good news.

"Great Spirit," Jibway said. "Holy God in heaven, thank you for this abundance of blessings."

Addison knew why he stopped there. Asking for more blessings would have only tipped the good-luck, bad-luck balance scales even more out of whack.

Principal Characters
Holy Crusaders

Addison Freeman, spouse Mariah, daughter Hope, deputy town marshal

Mrs. Freeman, Addison's mother

Joshua Reedley, wagon master during Holy Crusade, son Maurice the Wiseacre

Otto Vogelsang, skilled builder, son Hermann

Preacher Larrimer, pastor of Found Grace Church

Gallant Argyl, mayor of Brotherton

David McTavish, town marshal, Son Charlie

Sean and Timothy O'Riley, twins

Orson Seiling, married to Lizbeth

Agatha Janson, deacon of New Found Grace Church

Kansas Residents

Jibway Jim, Ojibway Indian, wife Maybell Jim

Ziggy Hostetler, Runs wagonloads of supplies from Atchison to points west

Norb Bass, manager of the wagon train staging lot in Atchison, Kansas

Mr. Potts, owner of the trading post near Brotherton

Members of Caleb Cromwell's church

Dora Young, husband Eli

Others

Mr. Dobbs, agent of the Emigrant Aid Society

Walter Standish, wealthy, rabid anti-abolitionist

Also by J. J. Zerr

Jon and Teresa Zackery Stories

The Ensign Locker
Sundown Town Duty Station
The Junior Officer Bunkroom
A Ticket to Hell: On Other Men's Sins
The North

Stand Alones

Noble Deeds
The Happy Life of Preston Katt
Guerilla Bride
The Ghosts of Chateau du Chasse
Who Am I
COP Corner

Holy Stories

The Holy Crusade
The Holey Land

Book of Short Stories

War Stories